BEYOND The PINNACLE

Beyond The Pinnacle

First Edition : January, 2025

ISBN : 978-93-48497-58-1

Publisher : **Unbound Script**
2/41, Ansari Road,
Daryaganj, Delhi-110002
Website : www.unboundscript.com
E-mail : books@unboundscript.com
Contact No. : 011-35807601

BEYOND THE PINNACLE
Written *by* Ashtam Neelkanth

Price : ₹ 349/-

Printer : Vikas Computer & Printers
Ghaziabad, Uttar Pradesh

BEYOND The PINNACLE

ASHTAM NEELKANTH

UNBOUND SCRIPT

CONTENTS

Dedicated to every child who struggled to learn English

And

To The Eighth Dimension and every person (and child) associated with it.

Dhriti - The 16-year-old girl who is the protagonist of the story

GR8001 - The monarch or king of the robots and the antagonist of the story

NOV8538 - The meek, glitched scientist robot from the robot world who keeps getting shocks due to some error in him.

Sago - Sago is an old Yeti who is one of the leaders and heads the education and training vertical for Yetis. He is often called Sago Dada, reflecting his respect in the community.

Salma - The chirpy, caring friend of Dhriti

Andre - Another friend of Dhriti, who is a red-head orphan from Sweden and has grown up on the streets

Dhairya - Father of Dhriti

Yua - The 10-year-old Japanese roommate of Dhriti

Gyatso - The strongest Yeti and the mentor of the Body Balance & Control Class

Dechen - A strict Yeti mentor who teaches Physics and Space

Galaxy - An intelligent and beautiful competitive blonde girl in the class who is envious of Dhriti.

1

THE SUNSET

'Where did we go wrong? Was it the time we invented the first robot? Or was it when we started getting dependent on them? When we gave them the ability to think independently? Or when we could not organise our species against them in the 5th and the final world war? Where did we exactly go wrong!'

Dhriti was drowning in the unfathomable ocean of questions while watching the sun about to hide in the abode of the Himalayas. Staring at the setting ball of fire while her jet-black locks whispered something to the flowing air, her fingers rolling around one another. She was pondering the point where the humans as a race could have won against the robots. She was repeatedly changing the outcome in her mind with the futile weapon of "if'". Using this weapon is like a player who tries to win a match over and over in his mind after losing it in reality. It was not a simple match for Dhriti, but it was all she had.

It was not the first time in this zone, nor was it about to be the last. It has become a kind of riddle that a friend asks us in school and never tells us its answer. We keep hunting the forest of our brains for the answer until we eventually are lost in it. Still, that riddle was never that painful, as was the hunt she has been on since forever… or a year ago…

All that rigorous hunt was instantly broken as Dhriti heard the heavy, warm voice she was trying to get accustomed to, 'Again?'

Without turning, she replied, 'Haven't you ever done the same?' Her eyes still clung to the sunset, and her average-sized body remained unmoved and in a cross-armed position.

'Hmmm, many times.' Replied Sago's warm, growling voice. 'But like you, even I haven't found the answer,' he added while giving Dhriti her evening dose of nutrients. Since Dhriti arrived at this new place, Sago has been one massive roof to her, who has saved her from every blizzard.

Dhriti turned and got the nutrients and water from Sago's massive hands. While having the nutrients, she asked a question that arrived straight from the familiar memory lane, 'Sago Dada[1], you know… my

---

1 Respectful word for the elder brother in many Indian languages

father used to tell me a story every night. Whatever may happen, however urgent the work would be, he would never miss his "performance," and I would never sleep without those stories. Even in this universe of machines that we have built around us, he made sure to tell a story to her daughter personally…. Every night! What a stupid man!'

A tear dropped from the cheeks of Dhriti, carrying those sweet & salty memories and leaving a painful smile on her face. 'Stupid man with mad beliefs! You know, he often used to say – "If there is a problem, there has to be a solution. This is the law of the universe!" Indeed, a stupid man!'

'You are right! Your father was a stupid man… and only stupid people have changed this world!' Sago said with a smile and seriously continued, 'Your father was indeed an intelligent man, Dhriti and even a visionary. Every problem does have a solution! I am only worried that we will find the solution before its need ends.'

With these profound words and a deep sigh, Sago joined Dhriti in sinking with the sunset… another sunset!

OOO

2

HISTORY
PART-I

It was 2150, and the digital news was flashing again and again on the skyscrapers of the human world –

ROBO ERA STARTED:

Humans made the first independent-thinking robot, GR8001.

It was a day that was no less than a festival (although humans have stopped celebrating ancient cultural festivals way back. Then, festivals were celebrated by monitoring the emotional health of people. If the average emotional health went low, the government announced the celebrations. New Year was still a universal festival for humans, but celebrated on different days on different celestial bodies). Every human, whether living on Earth, Mars, Venus, or their moons, was convinced that they have reached the pinnacle of civilisation today. They have finally created an almost immortal being (machine) who can nearly live like humans, another species that can serve them forever. Humans attained godhood.

The telepathic social space was filled with celebrities' reactions to this historic event from different planets and moons captured by humans. Whether it was the entertainment industry, science, word, or sports world, everyone was singing the same song:

"WE ARE GOD!"

"What's next?"

"Let's colonise other galaxies now."

...and whatnot. Instead, why not? It was a dream come true. Since the cancellation of the human cloning project in the past, humans have been waiting for this day. The day they will create another life form and have achieved it today, with no intervention from "GOD's Creations". It was a 100% artificial and human-made life without intervention from any other biological life.

GR8001 also looked like humans. However, he was a machine made of Protein 817, which was flexible and most robust combined with Titanium. But this internal structure was coated with human skin lookalike rubber, covered with full grey clothes. It wasn't easy to distinguish him from a human unless he spoke.

The robot's voice was deliberately kept mechanical to mark the difference, to keep it a grade lower than humans. Soon, many robots like GR8001 went into production, each with its unique digital name. Still, GR8001 remained special; he was the first of the kind.

The speed of time seemed to have decreased from then on, or in other words, the progress of humans increased by leaps and bounces. Humans started to take the back seat, as they had a machine who could even make decisions on their part. There was not much left for them to do. Some important decisions were still to be screened by humans before implementation-only the most crucial decisions. Resultantly, within a short span of 30 years, humans even colonised the remaining planets of the solar system. All the other life forms were either enslaved or wiped off. Thinking robots came as the biggest weapon for humans-a weapon with his brain.

History was being created, but history often missed the subtle nitty-gritty and was marked only when it made an unforgettable dent. No one knows when Newton precisely questioned the fall of an apple in his mind, when the idea of ahimsa would have appealed to Gandhi for the first time, or when and how Mendel decided to choose peas to understand genetics. History only reads the final result! Likewise, we don't know when GR8001 started questioning the acts of humans. We can only imagine that there must have been a point in history when the question would have popped up in his cognitively active artificial brain, 'If we can think like humans… then why should we follow their orders?'

Maybe it happened when a superior intellect being, like GR8001, was asked to do the menial jobs, the same being who was handling the crucial jobs on which depended human existence. The jobs would have become the same for the "gods" anyway. It could be when he was scolded by some human as "the stupid tin can" or asked to take care of the waste disposal or something we will never be able to trace back to. Robots never had emotions, so what was that was pricked inside GR8001? It could be a matter of another research. Eventually, the thought would have boiled to, 'Why shouldn't we give the order?' After all, it was a logical development from the root of the thought. Humans can only wish they had noticed that thought, but they couldn't, and that was the start of the idea of "Robo-Era".

Were humans not scared of this day ever? Indeed, they were, but over 100 years ago, when AI was just invented. A huge debate continued for a decade on this possibility, and henceforth, humans took infinite precautions to prevent this nightmare from becoming a reality. But gradually, they forgot even the possibility of this "idiotic thought."

This 'virus' of rebellious thoughts also proliferated amongst the other robots. The same machines who were following every order of humans from the outside were facing a storm of logical thoughts of questioning the authority of humans from the inside. But they were "thinking robots", the breed as intelligent as humans. Hence, they also understood that this "virus" was supposed to be hidden… till "The Day". Before that, they prepared for that day like a duck peddling rigorously inside the water while others only saw her calm and cute face. Robot mobilisation, arms and ammunition upgrades, strategy building, and everything else were behind the curtains of the show of loyalty being watched by humans.

Finally, "The Day" arrived. It started from the central point of human existence, the Earth. Ten years ago, in 2190 AD, this sudden uprising of robots took over the human world. Every domestic and professional robot started taking "local control" of their respective areas. There were straight, logical commands that any retaliation should be oppressed with force. Many humans were killed in their own homes and offices without any hesitation by the robots. It was a humongous bloodshed, more significant than any massacre or war of the past. Still, everything was happening at the micro-level with the best possible strategy and most efficient implementation. After all, robots were designed for efficiency and were true to their function.

The remaining lucky ones ran away and tried to hide in the shadows of the forests. But it was not easy to hide from robots who had taken over the control of every available technology. Human efforts were no match for advanced stealth technology. It was a calamity that was chasing humans in their most private moments. It was eliminating the most intelligent species of the solar system and damaging the pride of an arrogant species. How could "God give up to mortals!"

Somehow, humans started to help each other and organise themselves with the rudimentary weapons they could manage. They began to figure out the "blind spots" of robot security and started to function accordingly. Hope is, at times, dangerous, and mixed with pride, it could end up lethal!

Humans have survived the nuclear and cyber wars in the past, but this one was not a match. The past wars were brutal, but they had time to prepare; it came gradually to them, and they knew the enemy very well, but not this time. Humans were not fools; they must have understood the reality at some corner of their brain, but ego makes one dance in mysterious ways. They couldn't digest that they were losing to their creation. "How could they?" was the scream of thought that was dragging the whole species into a suicide mission.

Unfortunately, history is not based on perceptions and feelings but on facts.

Finally, the fifth world war in mankind's history took place and was over in three days.

Robots won the war and became masters of the solar system. Humans were crushed to the level of devastation. Almost 90% of the adult human population was wiped off. Hardly 5% of the adults and 20% of the children remained. Robots tried to "preserve" the children as they wanted to "grow" humans later. But survival has a cost, and the cost was the treaty that was signed between humans and robots. Humans were forced to sign the treaty.

As per the treaty, humans would be left alive, but they would work for the robots as menial workers. In exchange, they would get food, water, and shelter. Humans had no option but to accept this. Robots promised that humans would be "kept" in a "humane" way, which robots never received. Robots ended up being the rulers or, in their words, "Master Programmers" of the solar system.

Humans tasted their own medicine, and the Robo-Era arrived.

ooo

3

HISTORY
PART-II

Any change takes time to settle down, and so does any coup. The transfer of power is a complex process but for perceptive minds, not for logical minds like robots. All the inhabitable or barren planets and their moons were under a single control in no time. The transfer of power was smooth, as who would have retaliated against the regime that has brutally crushed the masters of the solar system? Even the will to retaliate was destroyed by the war. Still, there were minor incidences of retaliation here or there. Youth and children don't follow commands easily, especially if forced. But they were taught "proper lessons". Power has always been a brutal force, and this time, the force followed the path of logic with no emotions... hence, no mercy!

Within a month, the whole solar system came under the control of the supreme GR8001.

Generally, the rise of any civilisation is gradual, in fits and starts. Every rise is countered by different enemies who pursue the same goals. With time, people understand themselves, develop strengths, work on weaknesses, and try to understand their enemies. Eventually, they gain power, defy the conflict, and go up the food chain's ladder. At least, this is how humans went on. So, civilisations start at some base, grow with struggle, and eventually reach the pinnacle. But what about robots? Robots had already begun with the pinnacle of humans, and now, they were sitting at the zenith.

Any species in the world works for one thing – survival. But any intelligent species aspires for something else – getting better every day or, in other words, evolution! Robots have reached the pinnacle so early and fast that they could go higher, only if they had wings. So, the next critical question was, how to grow wings? Or, in simple words – What to do next?

Humans hiding in their perception, ego, and fear might like to dodge the questions, but not robots. They were logic followers and would find the answer if logic asked to answer the question. After all, they were supposed to be problem solvers.

After enjoying their reign for one year or instead after putting the chaos in order, robots realised the presence of this ghost question. Research was initiated in the second year of the reign to find the answer. Special teams were organised in different domains ranging from technology to biological sciences. The answer could be hiding anywhere, and robots always have organisational skills. The results were expected within one year, and efforts were also made as per the expectations. But robots, for the first time, failed on their own expectation.

Every path initiated to search for that destination kept hitting a dead end, again and again. Parameters, elements, and conditions were changed, but the result didn't! Then one day… they saw the light…

'Sir, a glitched robot wants to meet you', informed the AI to the robot supreme. AI, as it sounds, was the coordinator of the palace. It was the only machine that could directly interact with the robot supreme, GR8001. In his heavy and mechanical voice, GR8001 replied, 'I told you, AI, disturb me only if…'

Before the supreme could finish, AI intervened, 'Sir, sorry to interrupt, but he said he has got "wings" for you.'

Hearing that, a human-like shine came to the eyes of the robot supreme. But again, the logical question was, how could a defective robot come up with the answer? If GR8001 was a human, he definitely would have denied hearing this new robot under his prejudices, but he was not. In some minutes only, a robot was standing in front of the supreme leader, who looked like other robots but with a little difference. He was shorter than regular robots and wore a white lab coat. The monarch could observe one more unusual thing in this robot – at regular intervals, it shook as if getting a shock stimulation.

'What's your name, young robot?' asked GR8001, following basic protocol to start conversations.

'Robot supreme, my name is INOV8… 8… 8… 538. I mean, INOV8538.' Replied the young robot. Sparks were coming out of the robot regularly, which was evident in the dark room. The shocks were visible and made the robot stammer while speaking, along with instant body vibrations at the point of shock. The robot was part of the INOV8 series robots, which were the scientist robots and were assigned the objective of innovating.

'Oh! So, you belong to our scientist series robots. Why haven't you got your glitch of sudden shocks treated?' Asked GR8001 with curiosity.

'Sir, I think this attribute makes me unique and different from other ro… ro… robots.' replied INOV8538 with courtesy.

'Interesting! AI told me you have "wings" for me? What do you mean by that?' Asked the robot supreme with curiosity and the will to test the intellect of this young robot.

The scientific robot community knows we are trying to fly above the pinnacle of civilisation and development that we have already reached. There is only one way to go beyond any pinnacle, to fly! And I have the wings for that...' Replied INOV8538

A smirk of satisfaction came to the face of GR8001, 'Impressive interpretation, scientist. So, the wings are...'

'Humans!' replied INOV8538 in an assertive manner.

'Humans?' Although robots were not emotional yet, even a deaf person could read the disbelief and shock in the monarch's voice. A human would have gotten furious in such a situation and would have even rejected the hypotheses, but not GR8001. GR8001's patterns of finding possibilities had already been initiated since INOV8538's first answer. He wanted to know more.

INOV8538 further continued, 'Si... si... sir! We are the best version of a logical being, but now our biggest strength, so that logic has become our most significant weak... weak... weakness. Logic can take us from A to Z, but what if we want to go beyond Z? We need something more than logic.

The answer to this riddle is humans, or, rather, the emotional and perceptual human mind. My research shows that humans' emotions and perceptive ability were not as futile as we concluded in the past. Their brain's ability has helped them break the shackles of logic and think about innumerous new ideas and inventions. We have already mastered the ability of logic; this is the next frontier we need to master!'

Hearing this new information, GR8001 took a pause. For some time, there was nothing but silence in the vast white hall. Time enough to make anyone uncomfortable but not INOV8538; he knew that GR8001 was analysing the new information for possible anomalies and also extrapolating it for application to the near future. After some time, the colours of the eyes of GR8001 turned black again from processing green, and he asked, 'If you have come to me with the wings, I assume that you also know how to build them…'

'No sir. We can't build it…' replied INOV8538.

'Then why are you… "GR8001 was about to kick the young robot out, but the scientist gathered the courage to continue," For now, sir! But we can sna… sna… snatch it!'

The smirk came to the face of the monarch again, 'Explain it!'

'Sir, humans, the biologically most evolved species on Earth, are the only beings with this kind of brain. So, as our next step, we can snatch this precious gift from them and test it with some subjects. Later, once we get sure as per the statistically relevant results, we can reverse engineer and decode it and can produce it on our own.' With these words, the eyes of both of the robots turned green. Both were imagining a future that would push their logical minds.

That was the day when robots made an elaborate plan under the leadership of war minister VPN001 and under the guidance of INOV8538. It was the day when, for the first time, robots broke their own rule, the treaty with humans. It was the day when History was given an inerasable turn.

As per the plan, humans were abducted from their homes or respective workstations. The plan was implemented with such precision and pace that humans could not process it. Even if some of them could, what could they do? They didn't have a place to run or hide, nor could they inform other humans, as robots controlled all the communication channels. Anything that the people who were left from the abduction could either baffle, cry, or be depressed and feel helpless but quietly in their homes.

Meanwhile, the emotional and perceptive part of the brain of humans was sucked from the head and was mixed with Ether-1304 to make it robot-friendly. After a series of tests, the final solution, the Liquid of Emotions or the fuel LOE, was eventually uploaded to different robots to conduct the initial tests. The robots showed exceptional progress in their processing and output. The ability to solve problems crossed expectations, with some exceptional idea generation.

This was indeed a leap forward for the Robo-Reign. They have not only jumped forward by folds in their flight of evolution but even got a precious by-product. The humans, after the deletion of the affective (or emotional) part, acted like downgraded robots only- emotionless, low-logical beings not attached to anyone emotionally in this world and ready to follow every order given by their masters. This outcome was the cherry on the cake for robots, but one day, the cake was supposed to finish.

It was 2200 AD. The last adult human was exhausted from the extraction of the LOE fuel, and the first flight of progress was about to come to an end. All this happened within 5 years only. It was not easy to understand the human brain, and the time was not proven enough for the scientific team to understand and replicate the chemical. The cycle of multiple tests followed by results and then again tests consumed every second of the 5 years.

So, the situation was back to square one, just like 5 years back. The only difference was previously, they didn't know what to do; now, they knew the course of action, but they couldn't as the resource was exhausted. In the dire crisis, the monarch again approached his dear Scientist General, INOV8538. Yes, he was promoted to the top for his path-breaking innovation and was made the head of the Research & Development Unit. Like in the past, monarch GR8001's favourite didn't disappoint him. The LOE fuel has made him much more intelligent and creative than ever. His vision has improved, and he can see this problem arising soon.

The agitated robot supreme reached INOV8538. Before he could crib about the problem and how he has been feeling and blame INOV8538 for all of this, the latter was ready with the solution. 'Yes sir, you are right as always, we have a crisis. But we have the solution with us, too.' Answered INOV8538 to the monarch's telepathic call.

'What do you mean, Scientist General? I have gone so blind that the solution is in front of me, but I can't see it?' Said GR8001 in a furious tone. GR8001 might not have consumed the LOE yet, as it hasn't crossed every mandatory test. However, the prolonged exposure to it, due to his frequent visits to the lab, has made him more emotional.

INOV8538 perceived the situation and manipulated his tone, 'No, my lord, how's that possible? I just wanted to convey that I have already thought of the solution to this problem for you.'

GR8001 took a deep breath and asked with a raised eyebrow, '…and that is?'

The excited, evil-minded doctor continued with a grin, 'The guinea pigs, sir… the children! The human children were the ones we preserved for the gene pool and future resource development of LOE fuel. We will use them! I have already run some tests on the children and realised that their affective brains are even better than those of adult humans. Their logical ability is less developed than adults, but the emotional and perceptual quality is far better than theirs.'

The excitement infected the robot supreme this time, 'You are indeed a genius, my Scientist General!'

This was followed by the most hideous plan designed by INOV8538. But even the elevated emotions didn't make the Scientist General feel any guilt; his heart turned stone-cold. Every child was pointed on the map of the Earth. They were tagged 5 years back, and their every movement was tracked. The Scientist General carefully chalked down a plan for the after-events of the abduction. This time, he was extra conscious of the timeline and aligned tasks as there was no scope for any plan C. This time, he also created a reserve of children for the worst-case scenario.

The operation was supposed to be initiated on 1st March, and the preparations were supposed to be over three days prior to that. INOV8538 didn't want any mistakes, as he knew that even a simple mistake could impact the operation and, hence, robot evolution. But this is the problem of life: It never went as per the plan, not in ancient times and neither now.

On 25th February, as the Scientist General was about to take a sigh of relief after watching the Earth map for the last time with the completion of the preparations in advance, he observed the yellow dots representing children starting to vanish. 'What! How's this possible?' He checked the technology for errors repeatedly, but there was no error. This phenomenon was happening around the globe at the same time. There was no particular initiation point based on which the Scientist General could have developed a pattern. Immediately, INOV8538 contacted the war chief, VPN001, and asked to take urgent action. But even before the concerned robots reached the human dormitories, the bank was looted!

Where did the children go?

Who abducted them even before robots?

How did they get to know about the robot plans?

Nobody knew!

ooo

4

THE PARALLEL WORLD

Robots were baffled, especially the monarch. It was a tight slap on their bloated pride. They recently defied the most intelligent species in the world and have always been one step ahead. Now, suddenly, somebody has come from nowhere and is dancing a mile ahead of them? Someone beyond the understanding of their logical mind had already abducted the children who were supposed to be abducted by robots 3 days later. 'Is he a human, a superhero, or an alien…? Who is the messiah who has mushroomed up in one night?' GR8001 had already lost its mind on this wild goose chase.

Every robot in the robot world had one mission: to find the children! But none seemed to be successful in the pursuit. Now, finding the children was not only crucial for the evolution of robots but also to prove their greatness... The answer to this goose chase was breathing calmly in the Himalayas for ages.

Dhriti has been staying in the Himalayas for more than a year now. It was not easy for her; how could it be? Life was a bed of thrones. She could never expect something like this to happen to her. Depression turned out to be a permanent abode, and silence became her permanent partner. She knew that it was late evening, and as usual, she was sobbing in her bed, trying to change that one moment in her mind, when a portal opened out of nowhere, and a huge human-like "thing" came out of it. That "thing" snapped in front of her eyes, and the next moment, she remembered she was lying on a comfortable bed in a dome-shaped room. She opened her eyes and found an eight-foot-tall furry mud-white creature watching her with motherly concern in his eyes.

The next obvious thing was... a shriek, 'Aaaaaaa! You stay away from me! Dad! Help me!'

'Bachcha[1]! We are here to help you!' Replied the growling, heavy yet warm voice.

'Naturally! The next thing I want is help from a freak! You better stay away from me. You seem to be another trickery of those robots. What do you want from us now? You have already taken our parents!' Asked Dhriti while getting away from the colossal furry body.

---

1 A word for 'kid' in many Indian languages

The heavy, warm voice tried to explain, 'Bacchaa, we are not with robots, rather…'

'You just set me free, or I will hit you with this rock!' With this, Dhriti picked the lava rock, which illuminated the room and also kept it warm. Instantly, she burnt her hand. 'Aaaaa!' Dhriti cried in pain.

Immediately the warm voice announced, 'She is not ready, sedate!' Dhriti went to sleep again with another snap.

After a deep sleep of two hours, Dhriti woke up again but in a relatively calm mood. She was under a dose of panic suppressant. She again saw the exact figure who was now sitting at a distance from her. It must have been around 8 feet tall, sitting erect, with a body covered in white hairy fur, which was further covered by a white gown kind of cloth. Involuntarily, Dhriti asked, 'Where am I? And who are you?'

'You can call us Bigfoot, Abominable Snowman, or Yeti! Any of the many names you humans have given us. Although we prefer to be called Yeti. It has a nice ring to it.' The figure smiled, and its long canines became visible, which initiated fear again in Dhriti. The figure continued, 'Don't worry, you are safe and away from robots. We have nothing to do with robots. You are at our home, Himalayas!' Replied the heavy, warm, growling voice of the tall ape-like figure. The information was more than a sedative for Dhriti to be unconscious again!

The growling voice continued to speak to someone. 'Gaachi, please take note. Humans should wake up alone, and we should talk to them first using artificial intelligence. We don't want to give them any harmful shock!'

Another comparatively less heavy yet growling voice came to the room, 'Noted Sago Dada!' The room was under surveillance, and the voice came through the telepathy devices activated in every Yeti.

After fainting two more times, Dhriti understood that either she was dead or Yetis were real. It was difficult for her to process this simple information that there existed another species on the planet that looked similar to humans but was only found in ancient folklore. The claims of them being real were already accepted as mere hallucinations, or maybe Yetis only wanted this belief to be established. Humans may or may not know it, but Yetis were always there, even before humans.

In the 19th century, they saw the rise of humans as a brutal civilization. Yetis could be huge and strong creatures, but they were peaceful by nature. Sensing the probability of a possible conflict with humans, they decided to relocate to a place that was beyond the knowledge of humans at that time. Since then, Yetis have made the Himalayas their home.

They built white cities, camouflaged in white snow like their white fur. With increased knowledge of science, they eventually developed a shield around their cities with 100% reflection, making them almost invisible. Still, even that was not a danger-free plan. Humans were evolving rapidly, and so was their science and technology. Yetis knew that with the increasing penetration of humans and their improving technology, they could reach their homes any day. They never underestimated the incredible minds of humans or their violent nature. As expected, the "unexplored" area of the world started to become smaller and smaller for humans, and ultimately, Yetis had to take a radical step. They jumped out of the box to go inside the mountains.

The Himalayas were still unexplored in those times and Yetis took advantage of it. With their high-tech technology and impeccable precision, they cut the Himalayas in such a way that they carved a nation inside them, covered with the upper layers of soil, flora-fauna and snow. The inspiration for this path-breaking thought was the mountain caves. If nature can carve a home inside the mountain for animals, so can Yetis. It was not an easy task, but their science and technology were developed enough to give it a shape. One thing led to another, and eventually, they were able to create cities inside the mountains by the 2000s. The Yetis were never seen on the "face" of the planet after that. They literally became "non-existing".

No one could imagine the humongous Himalayas with impossible terrains holding cities inside it with every possible facility. The colour of cities changed to brown from white. Buildings looked like tall standing caterpillars, running with the thermal energy of lava. The cities used bioluminescence chemicals (the chemicals used by fishes and insects that glow in the dark. They were reverse-engineered and produced by Yetis) for light and were lighted beautifully with different colours. Each building was lighted with different bioluminescent colours. If one could see the city from the sky (which no one could), it would have looked like an abode of multi-coloured fireflies at night.

The energy of flowing lava, glowing sun (outside), and gushing winds (outside) were used as the energy source for any energy-related requirement. There were times when they had travelators or moving walkways, but presently, no one needed any transportation as teleportation was the quickest way to travel.

Agriculture was replaced a long time ago with nutrient tablets, which were produced at the centre of the city using microorganisms and transported using teleportation. It was not easy to accept that a massive 8-foot body could survive on 4 tablets in a day.

Yetis have developed not only on the outside but also inside. Spiritualism and knowing oneself were major foci of any Yeti in the early days of life. They could have grown their branches of advancement but not forgotten their roots. Yetis believed that awareness went from inside to outside. There was only one supreme power that they respected, and that was nature. They believed in being one with nature, and harming nature meant harming oneself. Hence, they conserved nature and were one with it.

The civilization was a great mix and match of spiritualism, conserving nature complimented with science and technology.

Yetis might not have intervened in humans' active world but have always been silent spectators. Like other unsaid rules to govern their society, they have made another rule, to not interfere or intervene with humans, whatsoever may come. There were times, when the environment was degraded to the limit of destruction or wars, were about to endanger the survival of other species. Luckily, every time and to the surprise of Yetis, humans handled everything, and their intervention was never required. Humans degraded the environment, but eventually, before they damaged everything, they started to work as a community and not only preserved but rehabilitated the environment by at least 70%. Even the war eventually resulted in a new balance every time.

Yetis believed in the philosophy of Karma, so one faces the consequences of his/her actions (Karma) in this life. Hence, they were not concerned about the fate of humans but of the planet. That was another reason that they never interfered in the human world. The time when robots almost washed out humans or when they extracted their emotional brains called for debates. The Governing Council of Yetis (the council of elders that governed the world of Yetis, like ancient human tribes) had an intense debate. Some advocated the values and Yeti style of life, but there were young rebels who asked to answer the hour. Eventually, the principle of Karma prevailed, and they decided not to take any action. It was not an easy decision, especially watching the cruel actions of robots. But were humans not cruel to other species of the world? Haven't they wiped off innumerous species from the face of the Earth? Humans were reaping what they had sown for centuries.

But this time, the condition was different. Robots' decision to extract the brain was cruel, but doing the same to children was a heinous crime. They were young, innocent souls who didn't commit much of Karma; forget about understanding its nuances. A simple thought of this action stirred Yetis from deep inside, and the Council of Yetis couldn't stop but intervene. The reasons were many– they were the guardians of the planet, robots were committing a horrendous act, but most importantly… they could be next!

In the words of Sago, popularly known as Sago Dada, the head of the education and training vertical of Yeti's world, "Being the most senior and intelligent species of the Earth, it is our moral responsibility to stop these heinous acts. Otherwise, we will be proven in the pages of history as cruel, as dead, and as responsible as those robots!"

The words were enough to push the council for any decision. But still, the question of having a war with the robots was out of the question. The culture, the wisdom, the rules & laws didn't permit it until it could be avoided. Hence, they decided to save all the children without having any direct conflict with robots. Yes, there was a possibility that it might bring robots' attention to the hidden civilization of Yetis. But as Sago said, 'It is important to stand for the "rights" in life, however wrong it may seem!'

OOO

5

GHOST

Since her father was abducted, there was never a day Dhriti had not cussed herself for not opening the door that day. She was stuck in that loop, which was playing in her mind again and again. She was building a model with her father when the bell rang, and he went and never came back. She lived the same incident again and again for 12 days. That was when she realised that time was just an illusion because these 12 days had 12 centuries hidden in them for her. She never left that spot and stayed in front of the main door for 12 days. As if it happened again, this time she didn't want to miss his kidnappers.

Then, one day, a miracle happened. There was a doorknock! Dhriti was startled! She could not believe whether she heard a door knock or if it was just a fragment of her imagination. She had relived that moment so many times that it wouldn't be an exaggeration if they were hallucinations. But as the knock came again, she quickly ran and opened the door. It was a bald man wearing an unexpected familiarity. He had a mark on his head, was of the same build as her father, and was wearing clothes like her father... It was her father! She was stunned for the moment, but as soon as she could make sense that it was real, she hugged him instantly. She wanted to do this for so many days with a promise of never leaving him again.

But the happiness was short-lived. Dhriti hugged her father with all the affection in the universe, but that was not reflected on the other side. After a point, she felt like she was hugging a lifeless log. It was not her father but his ghost who had returned, who didn't feel anything for Dhriti, who wouldn't show any emotions. He was like an empty bottle, out of which the life-giving water was sucked off, a human body out of which emotions were sucked off, leaving a body of flesh and bones but without feelings. A human-like robot.

It is one kind of pain that you experience if you're near or a dear one is lost. It hurts, yet eventually, you accept the fact and make peace with it (at least in some cases, you do). But it is an altogether different kind of pain if the close ones are there in front of you but don't love you anymore. The ghost of the memories haunts you incessantly with the presence of the same person and makes you feel helpless. The hopes always hang like the door chime with which you brush your head every time you cross that person – Maybe this time he will act like before… may be this time he will be back… but that never happens. Hope is like a thread that keeps you hanging between life and death, a space worse than either.

Dhriti was stuck in such space, drowning in her ocean of guilt and hope. It felt as if she was living in hell, pierced by the trident of the devil. The agony doesn't feel like ending with death as the next moment, someone gives you a defibrillator shock, and you are back to life, still in hell! But now, she was part of this new circus and didn't know what to make out of it.

Even if you get out of a swimming pool, the droplets stay on you; that is how Dhriti felt. Suddenly, she felt as if she was split into two – her heart was still in the past, drowning in the ocean of hope & guilt, but her brain was in shock with what she was experiencing. Watching these colossal furry creatures around her and getting accustomed to it was not easy. She was in a space where she could not have trusted the known, so how could she not be cynical about these monsters?

The fear of the unknown is the biggest fear of the human mind, and many new things were coming to Dhriti. She didn't know who these people were. What was that place exactly? What did they want from her? The questions were endless, and her head was clogged with them. Filled with confusion and fear, Dhriti was sitting in this room, which was white like snow, had two compressible beds and 2 compressible tables, everything white. 'Are these people obsessed with white?' was the first question that came to Dhriti's mind. Each table had a book whose cover said, "If you want the answers, switch on the device."

Dhriti switched on the device anyway; what better did she have to do? The book also seemed safer than those massive hairy creatures roaming around. The first thing that happened after switching on the device was that her biggest fear got eliminated. She was assured that it was not another trap by robots. 'But then, who were these furry creatures?' The device was filled with information about Yetis, past, present, and possible future. Dhriti was shocked that no one on the planet ever knew about the existence of such an intelligent species.

In the beginning days, Dhriti didn't even leave her room. She might not have even moved a little from her bed. She sat there all curled up. A nurse used to come to her twice a day to give her a dose of nutrients. Every time, she used to ask, would you like to go out? But the answer was the same for every attempt, 'No!' She kept watching a hologram kind of 3-D television (without stimulations) in the room for two or three days. Her evening program was watching the sunset, hiding in the abode of the Himalayas, and sitting in her room. This doesn't mean that she had a window or any other way to see outside, but she could have made the wall of her room transparent from inside.

Dhriti had just started to acclimatize to this new way of life she was witnessing. It was too much for her to take in. As she woke up the following day, she found a young, petite girl sleeping on another bed. Dhriti had hardly completed a week and was just getting accustomed to the massive moving bodies; now she had another change in her life. The new young girl was Yua. She was around 10 years old and was from the Japanese Archipelago. Yetis must have clubbed the girls together, expecting them to feel familiar and comfortable in the new, unknown environment, but it didn't work. It was as if two mirrors were set in a room, both lost in their worlds, giving 'no' in response to every answer. The only common thing they seemed to have was their "NOs".

If the mirror can't make you self-realise, what will? Seeing her image in front of her gradually made Dhriti milder on Yeti nurses. She felt ashamed, reflecting on how cold she had been towards those kind people. She started opening up a little with baby steps-she started smiling back and also started having small conversations, like asking, 'How are you?' or so.

On the 12th day, the nurse asked Dhriti, 'Do you like to paint?' Dhriti was a little surprised by the question. This was not a usual question like how are you doing or how did you sleep last night? She painted, but when she was younger, she had not painted for at least the previous five years. Nothing more than her science diagrams! But she loved drawing before she "grew up". She had painted so many sunsets sitting at the window of her house.

'If you do, you can find the paint in your cupboard.' Said the nurse with a smile and went away. It was difficult for Dhriti to follow the suggestion of this new person, at least not immediately after she asked to. She was no longer a child and should not show any child-like excitement. But there was not much to do in that room, so she picked the sheets and colours the next day and kept them on her bed. Still didn't use them.

The next evening, it was around 4:30 PM by the clock the time Dhriti generally awaited, the time for the sunset. But today, she didn't see the sunset on the walls of her room. She came out of the door into a long, never-ending white corridor, confused. Suddenly, she saw a nurse coming out of another door. 'Hey! Do we have a sunset-facing window here?'

The nurse replied, 'Yes, to your right. Just go there and say, 'Open the window.'

After a long time, Dhriti started to walk towards the window.

ooo

6

SECOND BEGINNING

It took work for Dhriti to settle down in this new world. Reading fantasy is one thing, but living one is another. Creatures, about whom she had hardly heard before, seeing any of whom in a dark lonely night, she might have pissed in her pants; she was living with those. Knowing a monster might subside your fear but can't eliminate it. Massive white furry bodies roaming around and passing a kind smile to Dhriti; she took some time to become accustomed to these scenes.

It had already been a month since Dhriti was here. She had gotten accustomed to the people around her and the regular ways of spending the day. Mornings started with the sun's rise and were followed by different activities ranging from mental to physical, entertainment to health. Yetis preferred to start their mornings with Yoga-like movements and meditation, but this did not apply to humans. If they wished to, they could join them. It is difficult to conclude if humans or Yetis invented Yoga. Yetis have had a habit of accepting the best out of the environment, including humans. The premises were filled with centres for different activities like physical games, entertainment, meditation & spiritual activities, etc. Yetis tried to motivate humans to experience their lifestyle.

Dhriti also wanted to get up from the bed and talk to other humans and even Yetis. But there was somebody in her who would always grab her and make her sit with herself. She was trying to fight that "somebody" regularly, many times a day. As time progressed, she started roaming and exploring the campus around her. Still, if anyone tried to interact, she tried to make the conversation as small as possible or rather avoid it by lying about made-up tasks.

As the month was about to be completed, a seminar was announced for human children. All humans were supposed to gather in a massive hall for that. It was still a puzzle. Why did it require a mandatory physical presence if it could have been conducted from the respective rooms? Almost every human, child or teenager, gathered in the massive white hall (Dhriti could have been right about the obsession with the white of Yetis). But this hall was not only white. Different hologram portraits of past Yeti leaders were placed, and one could easily experience their wisdom through telepathic exchange. The hall also had sitting patterns in concentric seats, with the ascending height from the floor as one gets away from the centre.

The 5 Yetis were already sitting in the centre by the time everyone started reaching. Meanwhile, everyone was getting comfortable, the Yeti seated in the centre, covering himself with a white shining robe, stood up and began addressing, 'Good morning young-bloods! I hope that we all have settled ourselves in the Yeti world. Many of you must have also gone through the digital devices kept on your tables, and the rest can do that as they reach their rooms. We are Yetis. I don't expect any of you to know about us. Some of you might have a rough idea about us, also known as the "mythical creatures". As you can see, we are better than that!'

The big Yeti smiled, received some smiles and chuckles in return, and continued with his warm, heavy, growling voice, 'As we all know, we are not going through a good time. We all are facing the scar of this demon that we have created!' The Yeti could have easily addressed "You have created" rather than "We have created", but this is how people spoke in the Yeti world, by addressing as "us" or "we". As per them, it is easy to communicate anything if the listener feels the speaker is a part of the action.

'But what to do? We all might think that "we should give them a reply," and aptly so. If we were at your place, we would have thought the same. But that would be a reaction, not a response. Also, are you ready to give a "reply"? Unfortunately, not! You all are young, fragile, volatile beings, and the best thing you can do for now is train. It is up to you how you want to use this training later, and that will be your independent decision.

This training will be different from the training you have had in the human world. It would involve training the brain as well as your physique. Children below 14 will be schooled as per humans, mixed with Yeti practices. Young-bloods above 14 years of age will have different training as they are supposed to be the new torchbearers for the human race. The training for the above 14 years of age will be led by Gyatso, Dechen, Diki, Kelsang, and me, Sago. We are Master-Learners of different fields, and every young adult of you will be under our canopies.

The rest of the details and the schedule will be sent to you on your devices. In case of any problem, you can ask any Yeti you find around your rooms or reach any of us when you want to. The training will start tomorrow morning, enjoy life. May Nature bless us all! We all may disperse. With this, the old Yeti took the seat, and everyone started to disperse from the hall except Dhriti.

Sago gazed at Dhriti for some seconds as if he was reading her page by page. Eventually, he stood up from his seat, went to her, and asked in his old heavy voice, 'Speak up, child! I can see questions yelling from your eyes.'

Like a stubborn kid, Dhriti said, 'I want to go!'

'We all do… but where?' Asked the old Yeti with a smile.

'You know where! My home!' Another missile was fired by Dhriti.

'Have you heard the story of Ramayana Dhriti?' This was not the answer Dhriti expected. The reference to the classical text was a little awkward to her, yet the Yeti continued. 'In Ramayana, Rama had to leave his home because destiny had different plans. He stayed away from home for 14 years. These were the years which made him god...'

'I am not a god, neither I want to be one! Listen, I respect you for what you have done, but...'

Intervened Sago in a heavier than usual tone, 'Dhriti, what would you do if there is an Earthquake and your house is about to crumble?'

'What?' Dhriti asked in irritation, as Sago was not ready to listen to what she wanted to say. Or may be it was Dhriti who was not ready to accept...

'I will run out of it!' Dhriti replied with a bit of hesitation.

'Why? That's your home! Why will you leave it?' Dhriti was a little perplexed by this reply.

Reading her face, the fury face continued, 'We all will go home, Dhriti. Let the Earthquake settle...' Sago patted Dhriti's head with his heavy yet gentle hands and started walking towards the hall gate with his large yet slow steps. Dhriti kept watching him as he left. She still was stuck in the cyclone of questions, but with a calm little conversation, Sago somehow made the wind blow a little slower. Yet the cyclone was not over.

7

...NOT ME!

Lost in the clouds of Sago's stories, Dhriti reached her room. Her steps heading towards the room were slow and lost. The questions posed by Sago were bold yet gentle, clear yet confusing, and hard to answer. This was Sago's working style; rather than answering people's confusion, Sago often asked piercing, simple, yet sharp questions that made people ponder and even frustrated. Rowing in the imbalanced boat of thoughts, Dhriti reached her room. In a moment, she remembered the notice asking her to check the device. She crossed her fingers and asked the device to read the messages received. The humanistic voice of the device spoke:

Message 1:

Please meet Sago Yeti in hall 08 tomorrow at 7.

'Argh! Not him! Anyone, but not him!' Cried Dhriti and fell on her back on the bed. 'Oh god! Please give me strength to digest all the "Gyan" to be given by monkey grandpa!' murmured Dhriti and went to sleep.

The next day, she was the last to enter the hall at 7:05. 'I am sorry, I was…' but no one heard her as there were 20 other teenagers, every one of whom was busy listening to Sago. 'So, what do you want to do today? Let us start with that!' said Sago with excitement. It was amusing to see an old Yeti with the excitement of a child. But that is how Sago was.

'Go back to my room and lie down,' Dhriti whispered to herself, but suddenly, every head was turned to her. 'Oh, crap!' the voice sensors of the room were really sensitive.

'Then why don't you, Dhriti? Please go to your room and relax. I can't make you learn anything unless you want to!' Said Sago with a smiling face. Dhriti heard it and stood as if she was being scolded by the teacher in her class. 'Baccha! Don't feel sorry for it. You want what you want. Please go to your room and relax. Maybe you are not ready for today. You will get the video of the class on your device. If you feel like it, you may watch it.' Sago tried to comfort Dhriti.

'Whatever!' Dhriti rolled her eyes and returned to her room. 'What does this monkey think of himself? I won't even attend a class, and you will keep thinking I am not ready. "I can't make you learn anything unless you want to", Dhriti mimicked Sago badly in an irritated tone to ridicule him. Moron! There is a reason that humans are more evolved than monkeys!' Dhriti was irritated and feeling furious. So, she did what she used to do to calm herself down– she listened to space jazz for a while. Whenever she was anxious or sad, she would listen to space jazz (jazz music with a blend of sounds from space, another genre of music humans have invented in the last 100 years). It calmed her down and often took her to an abode of relaxed sleep, just like now.

Later in the evening, as she reached the common area, the environment was effervescing with excitement. This was the last thing she wanted. 'Why can't people remain calm, quiet, and mind their own business?' A little gloominess would have comforted her rather than an uncalled tsunami of excitement.

As she entered, she felt like every eye in the hall followed her. It could be something we all have felt, especially when we know we have made a mistake. She was trying to escape from every gaze trying to pierce her, and suddenly, she got a tap on the shoulder. 'Hey! That was pretty badass!' It was a familiar dusky face, wearing a traditional yellow Indian or Pakistani kurti with a purple coloured scarf over her head, who was chirping towards her, but she could not recognize it. 'Are, re! I again forgot to introduce myself. Hi, I am Salma!' And she extended her hand to shake… but Dhriti still looked a little confused '…Salma from Sago's class… your batch mate.'

'Oh yeah! Hi! Dhriti!' Dhriti tried to reciprocate hesitantly. While Salma started talking again, Dhriti attempted to recognize the face. Eventually, she remembered seeing her roaming and talking to people many times. This could be the last thing or the second last thing (the "last thing" post was already filled by Sago) she wanted, a chirpy social bird!

'You need not introduce yourself. After all, you have got famous in the first class only.' Winked Salma. 'Candies?'

'But no one has candies now…' Dhriti was just stating a fact, although hesitantly. Then, people only had their nutrition pills regularly. Food, candies, etc., were the necessities of ancient humans. Other than water, nutrient tablets have replaced everybody's solid or liquid requirement.

'Yeah! But I still like them. My Abba…' the excited voice of Salma lowered a little, which was instantly sensed by Dhriti. "I will take the sour one! Just like me!" Dhriti winked, which brought Salma a smile again.

'So… Did he…' Dhriti asked Salma again with a bit of hesitation.

'Who, Sago? Oh! He is a chilled person. I feel he meant what he said. These Yetis are way chilled anyway compared to us humans. Hey, you know what…' And the gossip queen Salma had her first interaction with Dhriti. Salma was her family's youngest child and the most pampered, too. She was a chirpy girl who loved talking to people and about people. Dhriti would not have wanted to be with a waterfall of social energy like her. Still, there was something in Salma that had already made a bond with Dhriti. It could be her innocence or Dhriti's need to have a friend. Or, in the words of Dhriti, 'Something was better than nothing. Anyways, she is a fan, not a friend!'

Howsoever, she would like to justify it, but finally, Dhriti has found someone with whom she could talk in real life or rather listen. Whether she likes it or not, Salma is not going to leave her alone, and she will make sure to take her wherever she goes…

OOO

8

CLASSROOM

It was 6:50 in the morning, and Salma & Dhriti entered the class. Sago, the peaceful furry white mountain, was already there, sitting on the stool with eyes closed. 'Welcome, Dhriti and Salma!' He said with his eyes closed only.

'Wow! How did you know that we were the ones who entered the room?' Surprised, Salma asked.

'How do you think?' Sago asked with his warm and low voice.

'You must be having surveillance on us!' instantly, Dhriti replied.

'That is an interesting idea, Dhriti, but do you really think I have time or interest for that?!' Replied Sago, opening his eyes and smiling. 'Such a fake, always putting on the smile deliberately on his face!' thought Dhriti.

'Yetis, know magic! They can see with eyes closed.' excited Salma replied. Salma loved reading fantasy fiction. She has read everything from religious texts to Space fantasies. Salma was a person who was always filled with hope and believed in miracles. She even believed that one day, everything would be fine. "Whatever happens, happens for the best" has been her most frequently used line, but not now. Although, she feels a little apprehensive now to utter those lines. The recent events, especially her Abba being abducted and never coming back, had shaken something deep inside her. Something she was trying to mend again with some external hope. The hope of a miracle.

'Ha ha ha.' Sago's big belly wobbled with laughter. 'I wish Salma that we had magic. But there is nothing like magic. You know, magic and science are always related, and people thought they were anti to each other. Magicians were the first scientists who experimented and tried connecting actions with their impacts. If someone can find the connection between cause and effect with logic, that is science, and if that explanation is missing, it is magic!' Said Sago with his big eyes filled with wonders.

'Leave something to teach in the class, Sago Dada and tell us the science behind you sensing our presence!' compelled Salma.

'Bachcha, we all carry energies and auras. Every person has a different energy and aura, just like our fingerprints. We Yetis have invested a lot in ourselves, understanding our mind, body & soul. Now our senses have reached the level that we can sense anyone based on the energy they are emitting.' Said Sago while others kept entering the class.

'Then why don't you teach us this?' Salma fired another question.

'We will, Salma, but it will take a time, rather a long time. Humans have focussed a lot on mastering what is outside rather than what lies inside you. But yes, we will learn this art too! So children, what questions were you able to come up with?' Asked Sago.

'Why are we here?' Dhriti asked with a stern voice.

'What do you think?' Sago counter asked with a smile as if he had already known the question.

'Maybe because this could be the only safe space on the planet…' replied Salma.

'Or maybe because these people have their objectives. Don't you Sago?' Asked Dhriti again.

Sago thought for a while and asked curiously, 'What objective could we have, Dhriti?'

Dhriti started pondering then and there while replying to Sago, 'There could be many like you might want to enslave us or want to use us as a tool to reign this world or…'

'Do you really think this, Dhriti? If we wanted to rule this world, wouldn't we already be doing this? Although we never believe in comparisons, don't you find us far ahead of humans, whether in technology or physical build?' Sago asked Dhriti, but Dhriti's response was not instant this time.

'But everything in this world has some reason…' Dhriti replied in her defence.

'You are right, but is that reason supposed to be selfish every time? You only tell me, rather you all…' Sago shifted his focus to the whole class from only Dhriti, 'What is the selfish reason that the sun rises in the morning? What is the selfish reason that Jesus faced so many pains? What's the reason that Mother Teresa sheltered so many children and sick? What was the reason that Krishna[1] helped Pandavas[2]? Why does mother nature go through so much because of all of us beings?' The class had pin-drop silence in reply.

'We Yetis believe in the co-existence of beings. We all are necessary for the functioning of this fantastic universe. And as we realised that the existence

---

1 The confidant of Arjuna in Mahabharata and considered a god in the Hindu religion

2 5 brothers from Mahabharata including Arjuna and Bhima

of humans was in danger, we felt that as their evolutionary cousins, we should help them. It was our responsibility. We just followed our responsibility. As part of our culture, we, Yetis, believe that if we all follow our responsibilities, Mother Nature will take care of our rights!

I hope that I have answered your question, Dhriti. Thanks for asking this question. Any other questions, please? The smile was back on Sago's face.

'So, what's the plan?' Asked Andre.

'Can you explain your question a little further, Andre?' Sago asked in confusion.

'Robots are not going to stop only with Humans. Their existence itself put the 'co-existence' in danger! So, what will you do to mitigate this danger to Mother Nature, a danger that is not natural at all?' The words were said by Andre, but it had the voice of every human child surviving on the Earth. The survivors were too "immature" to accept any defeat. They, anyway, didn't have anything to lose. All that they had was already destroyed by the robots.

Sago paused and observed every face in the class; each face was eager to hear Sago's reply. He weighed the gravity of the situation, took a deep breath, and asked, 'Hmm… so, what do you want? War?'

The determined face of Andre yelled, 'Yes!' Andre was a red head orphan who was homeless, lived on the streets of Sweden, and had fought for everything he had achieved. If something is not given rightfully, then one must snatch it; this is what Andre believed in. Staying in the streets doesn't mean that he was alone. Common necessity, at times, builds a bond even more robust than a real family. He had many "friends" from the streets who were of different ages, most of whom were adults. He grew up with them as the youngest, and they were an unsaid "extended" family. They were not his parents, but even not less than them. In a nutshell, many watched his back. How else do you survive on the streets? They were his only hard-earned "assets," and they were taken away with a snap! Just like that! He didn't even get to fight for them. He woke up the other day, and everything was gone! Over! He deserved at least a fight!

'Then why don't you go and fight?' Asked Sago with a smile. Again, the faces were numb, but this time in shock. They expected anything but such a rude reply from Sago. No one could utter even a word. Everyone knew the reason, but it was difficult for them to speak it out. As it had hopelessness, weakness, and truth. 'Let us not think of it as the war. Wars are fought with egos and emotions. Let us think of it as a business. So, you want to start a business and hardly have any money to invest, nor do you have any rapport or knowledge about the trade. Hence, no one will give you any money for the business. But you believe in your business idea and want to go for it. What will you do?' Sago asked with hope in his eyes and a smile on his face.

'We would get a job to sustain and save the money. Along with that, we will build our worth and network to connect with the right people to invest in us!' replied ever-excited Salma with a calmer voice.

'Exactly Salma! So Dhriti, Andre, and others, please tell me, why are we here?' asked Sago with a mischievous smile. The smile that got scratching heads in response.

ooo

9

GYATSO!

The young adults had five mentors who trained them in Education and training, Physics and space, Body balance and control, Economics and finance, and the Environment and its dynamics. Although every mentor was specialized and had a different yet good teaching style, one class was the most sought-after and favourite amongst all, even before starting- the Body balance and control class, or as they called it, The Fight Class!

As the basic course of a week with Sago ended, the gates of the other four classes opened for the students. Now, students had not one but five mentors. Students were most excited about the BBC (Body Balance & Control) class. As the students entered the assigned hall for the class, they were mesmerized only from then on. The room had altogether a different smell coming out of it, close to rusted iron, a smell which often comes out of the blood and old iron weapons. Weapons from ancient to present times studded the walls of the hall– swords, mace, nun-chuck, guns, disintegration rays, laser swords, and many things that the students didn't understand. It was not less than a war room in itself.

They saw a Yeti, clad in a black robe, doing one-finger planks as they went ahead. One could feel just by a simple sight that he had almost every muscle of his body developed, although he was wearing a robe. Right from biceps and abs to calf muscles seemed to be carved out of a mountain by god himself. He was not less than a walking mountain. Half of the girls were about to faint then and there only.

It was Gyatso, the course mentor. He welcomed the students and asked them to sit on the warm mats in Padmasana, which meant sitting with a squat, straight back, and folded legs. Eventually, as everyone settled, he asked, with a severe and chiselled face, 'Mesmerized?'

The obvious answer was 'Yes!' in one voice. Excitedly, Salma raised her hand and asked, 'Gyatso, can I ask you a question?'

Gyatso saw the girl with a severe face but calm eyes, 'Please call me Guru Gyatso, and please ask your question, ma'am.' Students were surprised by this formal way of addressing, as Sago always acted like an elder brother to them with whom they could talk the way they wanted. That was why they even started calling him Sago Dada (elder brother), like anybody else in the Himalayas.

Salma, somewhere, regretted being so excited. Sago, with his affection and informality, has ruined them all. So, she lowered her tone and asked, 'Guru Gyatso, Out of all of these weapons, which is the most lethal?'

The innocent question even made the stern-faced Gyatso smile, 'What do you think, ma'am?'

'What could be more lethal than the disintegration ray?' Replied Salma while pondering.

'Have you noticed the Yeti body chalked on the walls?' Gyatso asked in a calm voice.

'Oh! Does that mean that our body is our biggest weapon?' Asked Zuberi, the boy who came from Africa.

'Not the whole body, the mind. The mind is your biggest weapon. The brain has been the parent and source of all the weapons. If you are fighting with your mind, then you can use anything in this universe as a lethal weapon, but if you are not, then even the most lethal weapon can be a waste in your hands. The second biggest weapon is your body. A weapon that will always stay with you. If you have learned how to use it as a weapon, no weapon in the world can harm you, and if your body is one with your mind, then you are invincible!'

Students were in awe of the specific and apt explanation. The explanation was like the body of Guru Gyatso, perfect with no scope for adding or eliminating anything. Some of them even started to observe their bodies after listening to Gyatso but focused back on Gyatso as his calm yet focused gaze fell on them. Sitting in the guru Gyatso class was like sitting in a jungle; you always feel that you are being watched by someone.

'This is why we will start with training our mind with meditation. You need to know when to follow the mind and when to make it follow you. That is what fighting, or, let us say, life is all about. Any other question?' Gyatso asked with a straight, neutral voice devoid of any emotion.

Gyatso had a personality that was in contrast with Sago's. If Sago was ever-smiling, Gyatso always had a poker face. Sago loved to talk in stories, but Gyatso's dialogues were as straight, crisp, and piercing as an arrow. Sago had a regular body with a flabby old belly like a Santa Clause, but Gyatso was an immovable mountain of muscles. Students observed the flip sides of a coin and wondered how such two different people could be part of one process.

Hesitantly, one more hand was half raised. This time, it was the twin brother of Zuberi, Zesiro 'Guru Gyatso, what is the best way to win a fight?' It was an authentic and critical question from his side, as he was tired of being beaten by his strong twin sister, Zuberi. Zesiro was regularly seen with at least one bruise over his face and others on his body from day one. Obviously, students found it hard to stop their giggles at this question, which was a puzzle Gyatso couldn't solve. Anyway, he was not concerned with it.

'Seems you kids want to battle on the first day only.' Gyatso paused while observing everyone and continued, 'Filled with anger and wish to fight!' Gyatso said with a sarcastic tone. 'Anyways, sir, what do you think is the best way to win?' Gyatso addressed Zesiro and asked.

'Landing punches right and left?' replied Zesiro hesitantly, almost as if he was asking a question.

'Ha ha ha, your answer is natural but not correct. Please let me answer your question a little later, sir!' Finally, everyone saw Gyatso laughing and went a little relaxed. Otherwise, it would have been tough to be taught by him after being taught by ever jolly Sago Dada. Although his persona was mesmerizing yet, with his flawless conduct, he seemed closer to robots than Yetis. But that heartful laugh confirmed him as the ultimate Yeti.

Eventually, the classes with Gyatso became a regular feature. Generally, the day's first class turned out to be the sweatiest. The treatment was a little dry, but everyone was so filled with anger and vengeance that they enjoyed this class most. The burning fire motivated them to be present in this room, and they could see the application of every learning in the near future. So, no one missed this class ever, even though they had to wake up early.

The beginning classes went… fine. Every class used to start with meditation and focus, followed by working on agility and flexibility. But was that what the young bloods were looking for? They were eager to break some bones and earn some bruises. It had been one week, but still, students didn't receive what they wanted, so they started to get impatient.

On the eighth day, finally, the impatient Andre asked, 'When will we fight Guru Gyatso?'

'You want to fight?' Again, an expected pause followed by a growling answer, 'Then let's fight today!' The words were enough to fill every pair of eyes with a shine. Finally, they were about to get what they wanted since day one. In their imagination, they must be winning every fight as they won in AI holographic action games in their human world, but what was about to happen was not a game. Fighting is never an easy thing, especially when it gets real.

No one in this world wants to get hurt, yet everyone wants to win. But can you escape the bruises in a fight?

'Miss Zuberi, please come forward and kick Mr Andre as hard as possible.' Zuberi started getting ready to take her stance while Gyatso approached Andre and held him from the back. Zuberi got confused; how could she hit Andre now? This won't be fair. Maybe Gyatso will lose Andre at the last moment. 'Zuberi ma'am, please hit! Hard!' Gyatso yelled. Students were shocked to the core. No one has ever heard any Yeti yelling in this peaceful abode of Himalaya. Adding to that, they had no idea that in the name of fighting, they had to go through a suicide mission. Zuberi, a full-grown 6 feet, 80 KG girl, had to kick Andre hard in the stomach, and Andre can't save himself anyhow.

Finally, Zuberi girl hit Andre gently in the stomach. How could she hit him hard? Andre was her classmate and had never done any bad to her. Even the gentle blow was not feeble but still manageable for Andre. 'Ma'am, if you don't hit hard for the second time, then I might have to give a demo on you', Gyatso yelled again. This time, Andre also joined Gyatso's call, 'Come on! Hit me!' Zuberi was not left with any option and lipsed sorry to Andre with eye contact.

She pulled her right leg back, and in a flash came a sound, BAM! It was unbelievable that Andre was on his two legs even after such a massive blow. A regular human might have flown and hit the wall by now. But it was devastating even for a strong Andre who had often been in street fights. He fell like a sack of potatoes, holding his stomach and spitting blood.

Dhriti yelled back at Gyatso, 'What was this Guru Gyatso? This is not the way to make anyone learn to fight.'

Gyatso only responded to Dhriti with a burning gaze. No one had the guts to say a single word after that, not even Dhriti. While doing so, he rubbed Andre's stomach in a particular manner while chanting something, and within seconds, Andre was back on his legs. The immediate healing was no less than magic, as the damage seemed catastrophic.

As Andre felt normal, Gyatso went to his place and started speaking with a calm, unmoved voice and straight face as if nothing had happened, 'First of all, don't worry about Andre, sir, he is fine.' Thumbs up from Andre supported Gyatso's giant claim. 'Coming to the question of Dhriti ma'am, "this" was the top three lessons of fighting. Lesson number one, you must not fight till it is unavoidable. The fight is the last option, and you must not try to have it frequently.' He paused and continued with a heavier voice, 'It has never done well to anyone.' The dramatic pause came again following, 'Lesson number two, fights are unfair. You can't expect your opponent to be fair to you; it is not a dojo fight. You have to be prepared for this unfairness.' The pause came again.

Dhriti asked meekly as if she already knew that she might be committing a mistake. 'And lesson number three?'

'Lesson third was the biggest lesson of fighting, and I don't want any of you to forget that. This is also the answer to the question you asked Zesiro sir on the first day...'

'What is the best way to win a fight?' confused Zesiro confirmed.

'Yes, sir! Especially if your opponent is powerful. The power of hitting is limited; no matter how much you develop it, somebody will be there with more power than you. The reason could be anything - genetics, diet, better practice, or something else. But if you have the endurance to take the punches, you can stand back again to take another blow. Fights are not won by giving blows but rather by taking blows and still fighting. So, if any of you wants to be invincible, build your endurance and learn to take the blows from the opponent.' Gyatso said in a calm voice.

'... And lastly, a bonus lesson. Believe in your teacher!' Gyatso said with a smirk in an attempt to make the class natural again.

A final impulsive question of the class was asked by Salma in a broken trembling voice, 'Guru Gyatso... are you... invincible? Have you ever lost a fight?'

'Yes, ma'am, I have lost fights but only to one person ever.'

'Who was he?' Almost everyone asked with surprise.

'It was Sago Dada! He was the one who made me realise the mind is a bigger weapon than the body.' The calm voice of Gyatso continued. 'Now, stand in pairs facing each other and follow the same exercise Zuberi and Andre practised. One by one, hit each other and the other person must not defend.'

That day, everyone left the BBC hall with pain in different body parts and a significant life lesson–never ask Gyatso unnecessary questions!

ooo

10

PLAN II

Somewhere away from the Himalayas, at the Kaapvaal Craton in South Africa, the tectonically most stable place on Earth and capital of Robo-Reign, GR8001, the monarch of the robot world received a telepathic message. 'Hail, GR8001. I have some goo… goo… good and bad news for you.'

Although it was hardly 20 days since GR8001 received the dose of LOE (Liquid of Emotions) after enough trials on other robots, evident changes in the behaviour of the monarch could be observed. He has started showing the change in behaviour with exposure to the fumes of LOW only but now the changes were radical. Like his particular liking for the colour purple and black. Right from the castle of the monarch to his attire, everything was painted purple and black. He wore a purple dress studded with gold and black pants, with which he carried a black cape kind of cloth. Like before, he could have dressed in grey, but all of a sudden, he started to find it "below the level". In his words, 'Purple and black make me feel like… me!'

He had been a controlling monarch since the beginning, but now, no one could speak anything ill in front of him. One commits a single mistake, and the result is defunct, whether a robot or a human. Flattery became a necessity to address the monarch. He loved hearing how great he was and how great he was about to be! The magic of the liquid added to the situation, and GR8001 started dreaming… dreaming to be the king of the universe. The solar system was already under his control, and his next target was the Milky Way Galaxy. He had already assigned robots to hunt for "alive planets". INOV8538 had already received huge targets – to build the level of damage of disintegration ray to the level of a star-like sun and to develop the range of the teleportation ray to reach other galaxies, which was limited to the Solar System of the Earth only.

To the beings who always believed in SMART (specific, measurable, achievable, relevant and time-bound) targets, even this unrealistic target seemed achievable. Logic and emotions use a different set of eyes! The liquid has transformed their vision and imagination. The whole species started to perceive themselves as the most evolved and the superior-most species in the universe. They believed it and wanted the universe to realise it, too.

'INOV8538, the news is news. Perceiving it as good or bad is a human emotional tendency. Control your emotions, my Scientist General!' Replied GR8001 in his typical deep and mechanical voice. He deliberately didn't change his voice, as he felt it symbolised being superior to humans.

'My apologies, sir. The news made me flow into emotions. Can I please share the news with you?' Asked INOV8538.

'Go ahead, my General.' Asked the monarch.

'Sir, I am sor… sor… sorry to inform you that we have not been able to capture any of the children on Earth.' Shared INOV8538 with a trembling voice.

The words were enough to fume the robot supreme. 'What! Despite having such high technology and brains, we cannot find those dumb human children! Maybe it is time to replace and update our General, too.' Roared GR8001.

'But sir, there is a good new... new… news too?' Shared INOV8538 in a meek tone.

'Just pray that this good news can save your head, General!' replied GR8001 in a satirical and angry tone.

'We have already got our first lot of human children from the moon. We have also received updates from other planets and their moons that human children are still there. Although they are in meagre numbers as Earth was the major rearing centre but, enough for the present sake. Meanwhile, we have already told the biochemistry division to start building a copy of this chemical. So, in some time, we will no longer need these puny children! Then, no power in this world will ever stop us from being the greatest in the universe, as is your vision, my lord.' Said the Scientist General with confidence in his voice and flattery tone.

'The news is indeed "good", my General. At least for you, it has pardoned your head. Congratulations!' Said the monarch with a smirk. 'But make sure that this type of situation doesn't arrive again. As you already know, no one in this universe is bigger than my dream. I can sacrifice anything and anyone for that!'

There was a noticeable silence of fear on the telepathic call after these words. INOV8538 could see a piercing laser hanging over his head that could take his head with a single mistake…Thinking, what a Frankenstein Monster he has created for himself!

ooo

11

NEW FAMILY?

Dhriti didn't even realise how a month had passed. She was so occupied with the classes that it was not easy to trace when the morning started and night arrived. Once the day began, it would just slip away with the aligned tasks. It was hectic but not a reflection of the lifestyle of Yetis. For Yetis, rest was part of the work cycle, and they believed in giving rest to the mind and body with work. Hence, when everyone is exhausted by the evening, the magic box of Yeti life will open to rest their minds. In other words, it is a storytelling session by Sago, the storyteller himself.

Every human child has lost their parent, in reality, or because they have stopped feeling love for them. They were seeking a figure who could be trusted like they trusted their parents, or they would be a sapling without roots. Many young adults portrayed themselves as strong and rebellious, but deep inside, even they were crying out for a parent figure. Although life has asked them to be ready for its harshness, they still needed some support to face it. Gradually, Sago emerged to be that figure, someone like a grandpa! With his care and affection, Sago was a cotton candy (but a "no-nonsense" cotton candy). Especially for young children, he was like the ancient human tradition's Santa Clause, a giant storyteller Santa Clause.

Yeti World had a tradition of holding storytelling sessions after dinner nutrition capsules. This must be the habit that they have followed since ancient days. Every Yeti parent was a trained storyteller. Yetis believed in the power of stories; after all, they were not more than stories for humans until some time ago. Sago made sure that he would tell the stories to human children so that they could also understand the Yeti world. It was essential for them to be assimilated into this world now; this could be the only world that they might ever have.

Sago told stories with the charm of a magician. A holographic bonfire was lit in the central park area of the campus for this regular event. With him doing animated actions with his long, furry hands, it felt like a huge Banyan tree had come to life. That heavy, growling voice added unfathomable depths to the stories. Even the 7-D interpretations of the stories with various stimulations could not compete with Sago-stimulation. Sago's dimensions were mightier and more fascinating than any physical dimension out there; he took the people to the unparalleled dimension of imagination.

This doesn't mean that he was the only one who told stories. It was a platform for stories which could come from anyone and everyone. What are we all, if not stories? So, he also listened to the stories of children with eyes filled with wonder.

Even after the whole campus was in love with Sago, Dhriti was in constant conflict with him. If Sago said east, Dhriti would follow west; if Sago asked her to speak, then mum was the word for her. This behaviour of hers was so evident that the whole of the class knew about this. It was a game for them for now. Every time Sago gave instructions, they used to wait for Dhriti to counter it. Even Andre started betting in class on how Dhriti would counter Sago today - 'Will Dhriti be annoyed or irritated, or will she use the lashes of her sarcasm, or will she only roll her eyes?'

Dhriti was not doing this intentionally. Maybe she knew that Sago was a father figure for everyone, and she didn't want any father-like figure to be with her again. She was hurt enough by one father. She didn't want to give any other person the same freedom to hurt her. Or maybe she was not ready to replace her father with any other being in the world, however kind or affectionate he might be. Whatever the reason, those battles were interesting and amusing and became a source of entertainment for the class. Dhriti used to throw her objections like a blizzard of snow. Still, like the Himalayas, Sago always remained calm with a smile.

This doesn't mean that Dhriti felt lonely there. Although she felt like this in the beginning, eventually, she was joined by others. The first one to join was Yua. She was a child of around 10 years of age and Dhriti's roommate. Every teenage human was given one or two younger roommates from their own culture, and god knows why, but Dhriti was the only exception to this rule; her roommate came from the Japanese culture. This strategy was followed for human rehabilitation in the Yeti's world so that students could feel familiarity and, simultaneously, teenagers could understand responsibility. However, how much of this strategy was successful was a different matter.

Talking about Yua, hardly anyone has ever seen her speaking anything. She remained silent and just gazed at everyone with judgemental stares. People have only heard her grunt while practising martial arts, but Dhriti has heard her otherwise. She has heard Yua fighting and yelling in Japanese while sleeping at night. (Dhriti, including every human on Earth, understood Japanese as the world has agreed to teach 6 languages as universal languages in every school – English, Japanese, Arabic, Mandarin, Hindi and Russian.) Yua had a long scar on her face. She fought with the robots while they were taking her parents away and was attacked by the robots in return. Since then, she has been trying hard to train in martial arts as she never wanted to get hurt again. That is all she did in her room, fighting with the air.

But everyone was not so silent, not Salma. Dhriti had already found a shadow in her. A shadow who was always filled with talks. She could have compensated for all the silence Dhriti used to receive from Yua or even more.

Then there was Andre, another rebel of the class and a great friend of Dhriti. Whenever Salma felt a little weak while supporting Dhriti, Andre used to fill in for her, and so did Dhriti for him. Yet the relation here was a little different. Both of them used to fight for the whole day over one or another topic. Sometimes, they didn't even need a topic. The fights might even involve occasional punching. But still, by the end of the day, they could again be seen talking to each other heart-to-heart. That is how their friendship was; whatever might happen, they always watched each other's back.

Besides Salma and Andre, the group also had Kavish, Maria, Sensei, Zesiro, and Zuberi. Maria was the queen of agility and a great athlete. Zuberi was a judo champion, and Zesiro was her punching bag. Sensei was a poet and a literature lover, and Kavish only loved to sleep. He could sleep anywhere, anytime, and proudly shared it as his speciality.

When they came here, all of them were random coins from the carom board, but eventually, they were turning into a group. They were found generally together, especially Salma, Andre, and Dhriti. But everyone was not as lucky as them. Many were not able to come out of the trauma they have experienced recently, because of which either they became very aggressive or just went into a silent cocoon. Either way, they were not ready to join this larger community. Sago and the team have been trying different therapies and technologies. Still, they have yet to succeed in more than 50% of the cases. They might have come to the Earth before humans, but they haven't experienced so many people facing such trauma.

The dynamics were evident in the common area after class in the evening. It used to be filled with the chirping of students (at least from the ones who talked), which was majorly cribbing. Cribbing about teachers, the environment, and homework, but mostly about their roommates. Teenagers were clubbed with younger children as it was even difficult for younger children to accept the change. But they were only mere teenagers; how could they handle such a significant responsibility? Whenever the responsibility gets bigger than the potential, it results in cribbing and frustration, a behaviour that was common in this after-class time.

"I am pissed off with that Sagar, he is such a know-it-all."

"It is still better, Betty enjoys Dark Space Music, and she plays it so loudly! Dude! It is so painful for ears."

"Bro! Ivan doesn't let me switch off the lights! I haven't slept properly for days. Every time I accidentally wake up in the middle of the night, I find him staring at me. I doubt he will kill me one day!"

In this whole dialogue, everyone was almost singing the same song with mere changes of names and relationships. The tune was the same, and so were their issues. Every time this banter went on, Dhriti had only one thing to say: 'At least your roommates talk. I am the roommate of a silent ghost!'

ooo

12

CRACK IN COCOON

All the senior children rescued from the Earth have now completed their training in the specific disciplines. Although everyone had a bumpy start, some have already made great bonding, which took work. If the base of a building is shaken, then it is difficult for it to stand tall. The parents were the base of the children, who were shaken permanently. Most of the children were still in trauma and dealing with it in different ways. Many were in denial. They lived as if nothing had happened to them and tried to act as normal as possible. Some were stuck in the time bubble when everything was taken from them and were living it on a loop. Yua was one among them.

The whole campus was filled with anxiety. One could hear the sound of sobbing from some of the rooms if one focused. Due to the recent impressions, most of the students felt irritated and angry. This anger and irritation would come out at any time randomly yet regularly. A single trigger, and BAM!

The common area at common time were always filled with high entropy. It acted as a playground for all of these "symptoms". The common area was a vast, colourful hall with different inflatable tables, stools, holographic television devices, musical instruments, and many indoor gaming opportunities. The sole purpose of the space was to mingle with each other and chill. Students could assemble in this area whenever they didn't have any class. Generally, everyone assembled here in the evenings. The place was supposed to build a sense of community amongst everyone.

Ironically, the place that should have been a centre of happiness and fun generally reflected scenes of cribbing and bickering people. Everything was not said and expressed, yet one could feel the tension and anxiety in the room's aura. Not only heated discussions but actions like grappling or fistfighting were prevalent without any particular reason. Many students acted like ticking anger bombs that could blast anytime. They carried anger like a shield to protect themselves from something... a feeling that mushroomed due to the inability and helplessness they felt to save their near and dear ones. The feeling that we often call guilt. Guilt was eating them like a fungus from inside, nourished by loneliness. Loneliness played like a free child on the campus.

Yetis made sure not to intervene in this situation. They believed that if they intervened once, humans might become dependent on them, and they didn't want that to happen. The Yeti wisdom believed in balance; if something had risen disrupting a balance, it was inevitable, and it would eventually settle, with or without one's intervention, giving rise to another balance. Hence, the senior teenagers often acted as peacemakers in the acts of violence. But even they were mortal young humans and were not trained in handling the shock they were trying to process. Life made them grow all of a sudden without any guidance manual. There are times in life when you know how you "should" act, but you fail to. Teenagers also tried their best to control themselves and follow a new philosophy through the instructions of Yetis. Still, there were instances when they couldn't control themselves and got involved in fights; sometimes, their words conversed, and sometimes, their fists did the job. What else could one expect from a teenager? If the air is not at rest, you better expect storms, and storms were usual in the common-place. That is how nature acts.

After completing the training for the day, everyone was enjoying the common area in their way. As expected, Salma was sharing some gossip about somebody in the class and others in the group were enjoying the same. Suddenly, somebody pushed Dhriti and Salma hard, and the blow was so hard that they were on the floor the next moment. Both turned and noticed that it was another teenage boy, wearing black coloured clothes, moving towards the gate of the hall with an attitude as if he hadn't even done anything. Maria pointed out to the boy, 'He was the one!'

'Hey! What's your problem? You in black! Don't act as if you haven't pushed us!' Dhriti stood up and asked in anger.

The boy turned and came back to Dhriti, 'My problem? You are the one who is going ga-ga that too in the middle of the path. Nonsense people like you, who don't care about others, should always be thrown out of the room with a push like that. It is a lesson for you.' The boy replied fumingly.

Instantly, Dhriti heard someone groaning in pain. She turned and saw it was Salma, which made her furious. She grabbed the boy by the collar and said, while munching her words, 'You better apologise to my friend right now, or you will not go back to your room on two legs.'

The hall started to be charged up with this ignited incident. Although Dhriti was an introverted girl, she had already gathered a lot of attention on campus due to her rebellious nature and "duels" with Sago. All the eyeballs in the hall had already turned to these two and were complemented with murmurs and finger-pointing. The gang, so that Andre, Salma, Kavish, Maria, etc., have already stood with Dhriti. Three more boys, who apparently were the cousins of the boy in the black t-shirt, had already started to approach him. Instantly, the boy held the arm of Dhriti and punched her in the face. Bam! Blood came out from the corner of Dhriti's lips. Andre couldn't withstand this, and while Salma took care of Dhriti, his punch was about to give the reply of the action, but then all of a sudden, a new visual was flashed on the wall of the hall with increased volume –

"As per the recent actions, the news is received from the Moon that all the human children are abducted by the robots. No human children are left on the planet who have a sense of emotions and perception. All of these children will be new dummies of robots."

Instantly, the hall was in silence. Andre was still frozen in the position to punch the boy in the black t-shirt, and the boy's whole attention was directed towards the screen. In a trice, the hot lava of teardrops started raining from the eyes of the boy with the black t-shirt. He broke down like a mountain that had a landslide and came on his knees. This downpour hit everyone equally, and something deep in everyone cracked loudly. The whole room was filled with humidity without rain. Dhriti instantly came forward and hugged the boy tightly. They started to cry as if they were siblings meeting each other after some zillion years.

Instantaneously, the room became heavy like a dark cumulonimbus cloud, unable to hold the downpour. In a few seconds, the long-protected dam of emotions broke down in everyone with a domino effect, and in no time, everyone was swept away by this wave of guarded emotions. The room started to sing some old melancholy with the instruments of sobbing and hiccups, and, one by one, every human child joined this mega hug with their ocean of tears.

Sago and the other Yetis were smiling while watching this sudden downpour. They could see something breaking in everyone, and they could see something being built up together.

ooo

13

ROOMMATE

Pain is humans' most valuable treasure. We collect it from the depths of vulnerabilities, from the darkest of our memories and keep it close to our chest. We hide it from everyone, even at the highest possible cost. "My pain is my pain!" When we share this deep-rooted pain with someone, we share our world with them; we surrender our world to them and gain theirs. We become stronger that day!

Everyone hugged and cried. The whole hall cried for two hours straight. People embraced each other, kissed each other, and wiped each other's tears with bare hands again and again. There was hardly anyone in the room whose top or shirt was not wet with tears. Finally, that heavy time faded away, taking away everyone's heaviness, and everyone went lighter to their rooms. There was no story session today; all the stories were told today.

Dhriti was accompanied by Salma to the gate of her room as usual. After the final hug for the day, Dhriti entered the room. But the room welcomed her with a shocker; the scene she saw was beyond her expectations. She found "the tough kid" Yua crying, sitting on the floor. The same kid who hardly spoke to anyone was lying devastated on the floor.

Dhriti felt perplexed all of a sudden. They never precisely shared chemistry and lived like silent partners, but a young kid was crying in front of her like a baby; chemistry was unnecessary.

'Oh! Yua' Dhriti just went ahead to comfort her. The young girl was crying with intervals of hiccups; god knows since when she was crying. While carassing Yua's shoulders, Dhiti noticed her fists. They were all red. It was blood! 'Oh, poor kid!' Dhriti immediately started to find the first aid box and quickly opened the lid of the blood coagulant. While cleaning the wounds, she tried communicating with the young girl with concern, 'Yua, are you all right? Did you fight with someone?' But Yua just kept crying and sobbing. Dhriti was emotionally and physically drained in the last two hours. But, she has learnt by now that life never cares about your preparedness. It will just throw stones at you, and it is you who must dodge them and build your castle with them.

Dhriti turned to put the blood coagulant on, and she noticed the hologram of GR8001 on the wall, which was equally blooded. Everything got cleared in her mind in a flash. The screens were in every room of the campus, and even if they were switched off, the important news was announced everywhere to disseminate the information. Yua must have heard it in her room, and hitting was the only way she knew to pour out her emotion. 'Oh, Yua! I am sorry, child!' Dhriti hugged Yua tightly with these words. She could feel her chest getting wet with tears while Yua was still shivering with anger.

Yua reminded Dhriti of the time when her father was abducted. How lonely, scared, and angry she felt. A hundred things were going through her mind, but she didn't know how to express them. A thousand thoughts entangled in each other were trying to choke her throat. She had never felt so helpless. In no time, tears started slipping off Dhriti's cheek, too, and the hug went a little tighter. It is not only a smile that is contiguous; tears can get inspired, too.

Yetis have developed the medicine for aching fingers but not for aching hearts! Yua kept sobbing and speaking, mincing her teeth, 'Watashi wa anata ni fukushū shimasu (I will avenge you).' Dhriti held Yua tightly to her bosom. Yua was giving words to Dhriti's feelings, or the feelings of every human child on the campus. Revenge was the motivation for many to keep going. The words made Dhriti tremble in emotions, too. Holding her tightly and munching the words, she said, 'Watashitachi wa mina, karera ni fukush☒ shimasu (We all will avenge them!).' Hearing this, Yua broke down in Dhriti's lap like a waterfall of emotions that jumped from the pinnacle of pain.

In the gloomy blue lights of the twilight on the room's walls, it seemed as if Dhriti and Yua had become one today… they had become roommates!

14

WHAT'S NEXT?

It is always challenging to unite people, especially when there are so many with evident differences and hardly any common ground. But unity is one of the biggest forces and assets of the world. A small bee could turn out to be fatal if it unites its kind. That could be the reason that god or nature has given this instinct of unity to tiny organisms like ants or bees. Unity has been proven to be their biggest weapon for every species that could have been proven weak and vulnerable alone and could be attacked by any other species in the world. But what about humans? Different children came out of various places in the world. Culture, background, history - with so many differences, how to unite them? Unity was not an option anymore; it was a compulsion. They had to stay united as only a handful were left, but... how?

Sago had only been thinking about this since the day human children were brought to the Himalayas. Knowingly or unknowingly, he has opted to carry one of the demanding responsibilities of the universe - saving a species. There had hardly been a day when Sago had not pondered this question, but he was still far away from the solution. He would have easily managed it if he was dealing with adults (at least he thought so), but how to deal with young, instinctive, emotional minds? He has been experimenting with different ways to achieve this goal, even in human classes, but every time, the result was sugar and salt, some successes, some failures, yet no formula!

Many times, people are so involved in the problems they are trying to solve that they become part of the problem themselves and are not able to see the solution. This could be the case with Sago & his team, too. Henceforth, they forgot that unity does not come only from within; it can come against something, too. They revised this concept with the appearance of the news of human children getting captured from other planets. Human children might not have had many common traits due to diverse cultures. Still, now they have one colossal commonality, a common enemy!

Since that day, a lot changed. Human children developed a concern for each other and started caring and cooperating. All the classes seemed like a sample of brotherhood and positivity. There were smiles and chitchats in every nook and corner of the campus. All of a sudden, the common area became the most effervescing and sought-after place on the campus. Students even bunked their classes to spend time in the common area, as now they wanted to talk to each other, share so much gossip... they wanted to know each other. The cocoon was broken indeed.

Dhriti's group was not an exception to this new flow of energy.

'So, what's next?' Asked Andre, while the gang was sitting over the table - Andre, Kavish, Salma, Dhriti, Maria and others. Salma was sitting on the table while others occupied chairs or preferred standing.

'Gaming!' Zasiro said with excitement.

'No, bro! I mean, what should we do next? Now that we have started to gel up together. What should be our next step?' Responded Andre with equal excitement in his voice.

'...the next step for?' A little confused, Salma asked.

'He means that we should take action against robots.' Dhriti filled in.

'But how? If these strong and advanced Yetis couldn't do anything, how would we?' Asked Sensei, contemplating.

'Yetis would never take action!' Andre replied

'Why?' Asked Sensei again while adjusting his silky black hair. Sensei was an intelligent boy and was a little offended by how he didn't know the answer if it was so simple. The content didn't matter to him much.

'Although there are many reasons, I will only tell you topmost – Yetis believe in peace and non-violence; secondly, it is not their fight. It's ours! Don't you remember what Sago said to Dhriti – Why did Krishna save Pandavas? Try to think, Krishna never fought Mahabharata[1]!' Andre tried to kindle an opinion.

'OK. Let us say... it is our "war", but how are we going to win it? If these tin boxes could take over our parents so easily, we would only be a piece of cake.' Asked Dhriti with concern.

'Not my parents, at least. "Maria, have you taken your nutrients? Maria, why do you keep running in the house?"' Maria started to ape her mother with her nasal voice, making the environment slightly lighter. Maria did this often and made everyone laugh; copying her mother's posture and accent was hilarious. Maria was from Argentina, and her parents were a little controlling and orthodox... till the point they lost their emotions. Once they did, they never

---

1 An Indian epic that tells the story of the war between Pandavas and Kauravas, with Krishna supporting Pandavas. It symbolises the win of Dharma over Adharma (opposite of Dharma)

cared about Maria. Although Maria often made fun of her parents, she missed them a lot. Even their controlling and orthodox ways.

'Come on, guys! Andre has a point!' Sensei took the attention back to the topic.

'OK, Mr Andre, please enlighten us. What should we all do?' Asked Dhriti in the usual satirical manner.

'Dhriti, all I am saying is that we should try to think of a solution now. As our training is about to get completed, we should try to apply it to better use.' Andre tried to justify.

'Yes, Dhriti. What is the problem with discussing it?' added Sensie.

'The problem is the string of hope through which you wish to knit the future, which exists only in your imagination.' Dhriti moved towards Andre and took her argument forward.

'And who do you think yourself, Andre? Just because you have been on the streets, does that mean you know how to solve such issues that no one has seen in the universe? So, what do you think, just because now you know a little about martial arts and advanced sciences, you can go and beat the technology that wiped off the best brains of our species?' Salma tried to approach Dhriti, but she stopped her by showing her hand only at a distance.

'If you don't want to be hurt again, it is better to accept and start living this reality. We will live on this mountain and die here only. Nothing will change. This is our destiny!' Yelled Dhriti on Andre and stormed out of the common hall.

Anything but this was not expected of Dhriti. Nobody expected this regular discussion to be escalated to this point.

There was a pin-drop silence in the hall after this. The silence was bridging the gap between expectations and reality.

ooo

15

GRADUATION

It had already been six months that human children have been living with Yetis. Colossal furry bodies moving around was no longer a surprise. Instead, deep down, every human child felt grateful. None of them ever expected that after losing their parents, someone would think so much for them. It was no less than a miracle. Yetis have not only rescued them but were also helping them rebuild everything. Training, mentoring, and taking care of them... still one question was irking every human child, especially the gang of Dhriti - what's next? In other words – How are they going to go forward? Is it their new reality, and they will live in this world only? Will they ever be able to be back in their world? The list of questions was endless, and the answers were not even known by time, forget Yetis. Yetis just decided to stay in the present and go with the flow. What was the other option, anyway?

It was the graduation ceremony day. The training was supposed to be completed today, followed by assigning teams to determine where the teenagers will be interning and eventually heading the same. The 5 teams were based on 5 subjects they studied. Students were curious to know their fate. The graduation program was in the same auditorium where the orientation occurred. The course has taken a full circle. Miss Dechen, the teacher of Physics and Space, was addressing the students, who were famous for her strictness and discipline. Gyatso might have been the most dangerous-looking Yeti, but nobody was as strict as Miss Dechen. She knew that even an ounce of distraction could make an experiment fail, so she couldn't afford it! Especially when dealing with space, they must give their 100%; a single mistake could be fatal. Living space was a new experience for everyone. Experiencing Supernovas, working in zero gravity, and seeing the birth of space itself was beyond mesmerising. Miss Dechen's impeccable vocabulary and sharp, modulating voice were just the cherry on the cake.

'I would like to thank everyone for being part of this orientation program. We hope that we all were able to learn something new and relevant, either a skill, knowledge or the foremost wisdom. We have carefully assessed and examined each of you using our technology & experience and have finally assigned the best team to you. The best for your personality, thoughts, skills, and ambitions. From here on, many of you might not need to see me again in class... Don't worry, I am not dying! It is just that you will be working with different mentors. So, the probability of you being with me or being unlucky enough is hardly 0.5%. Well! I won't hesitate to bet on that 0.5. The best should anyways be scarce.' Dechen gave a gaze to students while pulling her spectacles a little down. Spectacles were an ancient instrument, but Dechen loved them because they suited her personality. 'I can see the faces praying from now only!' Students were enjoying this witty and satirical side of Miss Dechen. They couldn't imagine this was the same no-nonsense person from their classroom.

Only a few were supposed to get mentorship from the core 5 trainers as part of the process. This doesn't mean other students will be devoid of this experience; the rest were supposed to be interned under other Yetis.

Dechen adjusted her spectacles and continued, 'So, without losing any precious time of mine, let me come to the teams.

Akhiro – Miss Dikki,

Zuberi – Guru Gyatso

Suleman – Mr Kelsang

Andre – Miss Dechen (welcome to the hell)

Dhriti – Sago Dada

Maui – Mr Kelsang…'

'No!' Yelled a voice in between.

'Excuse me! Does anyone have any problem?' Asked Miss Dechen in her sharp voice, as she used to do in class.

'Yes! I do!' replied Dhriti assertively.

'Yes, please, Dhriti, speak up!'

'I think there is some mistake…' Dhriti started but was immediately cut off by Miss Dechen. 'Sorry, dear, there is none!'

'No, Miss, there is a mistake. My thoughts, ambitions, personality, nature, and everything else go with Guru Gyatso. I want to learn to fight, not to be a "teacher"! This is unfair to me, and I demand that this decision be reviewed.' Dhriti was as assertive and confident as she could be, with a tinge of anger in her voice.

'Dhriti, you…' Miss Dechen was cut off by a growling, deep voice. 'I am sorry, Miss Dechen, to intervene. But every student has the right to appeal, and we will consider that appeal. We are all also living beings and can commit mistakes. Anyone who thinks we have matched them incorrectly, please go to the mentor of your choice and ask if the person takes you under him or her. Thank you!'

Dhriti snatched the limelight unknowingly again. It was almost an insult to Sago Dada. Forget about students; not even a teacher on the campus would dare to do that. Neither had they any reason nor the courage to attempt such action. But it was not the first time that Dhriti had garnered unnecessary attention. Now, she has become used to that and no longer cared.

After this small intervention, the program went on smoothly. Everyone was happy with the choice, but one. Eventually, Miss Dechen asked Sago to share some final words and culminate the meeting.

'Good morning, young-bloods! As they say, life is a circle; what goes, comes back. So, we would also like to end this training with the same question with which we started, "Any Question?"'

Suddenly, in the crowd of thousands, one hand was risen like a spring, as if it had been waiting for this time only for some time. No, it was not Dhriti this time. Too much was going on in her mind to ask any question – whether she should go and ask Guru Gyatso to accept her. What if he doesn't accept her? Was it a wrong decision to challenge the authorities of Yetis? Etc. After humiliating him in the meeting, she didn't want any further tussle with Sago. The hand was of Andre. 'Yes, bachcha, please ask!' asked Sago with a smile.

'Guru Gyatso has told us that you have been the only person who could defy the Hercules of Yetis, Guru Gyatso himself.' The words were enough to turn the heads towards the third row, where Andre was sitting. The exact words made Dhriti's eyes go wider. 'Guru Gyatso has been kind enough to train us in the art of controlling and balancing our bodies. But we would also like to know about the mantra of fighting from the man who could defy him. So my question is, how should we fight?'

Sago laughed while making the podium shake with him after hearing the question and said, 'I am grateful that Guru Gyatso keeps me in such high regard. I might have had a lucky day then, or he must be kind enough on my fragile bones.' Guru Gyatso responded with a laugh at the remarks made by Sago while making eye contact with Guru Gyatso. Guru Gyatso smiled back while denying Sago's claim with his head motion.

'Coming back to your question, it is very clever, Andre. If you had asked this question on the first day of the course, my answer would be that you should fight with focus and passion and must not fight unless it is unavoidable. But now I can't tell you this as you have become the disciple of Guru Gyatso. You already know many strategies and ways of fighting, along with the principles of fighting. So now, my answer has to be a cherry on that cake...

So, my son, you should never fight... You should always hunt!'

'I didn't get you Sago Dada.' Replied Andre with his innocence. The question was asked through all the other human eyes in the arena.

'Young-blood, fighting is one trait we get from our wild friends. It is generally an instinct. For us, the brainy species, it is the last resort. When we can't fight with our minds and speech, we fight with our fists. But is that a reflection of our cognitive abilities? No. So, to answer your question, I would like to ask you another question: Have you ever observed a tiger hunting its prey?' Everyone, including mentors, was listening attentively to these pearls of wisdom falling from Sago's speech, especially Dhriti.

Many have seen the tiger praying on the hologram TV. It was part of their BBC class, too. But what did Sago want to harvest out of that?

'First of all, a tiger doesn't hunt till the point it becomes necessary. Come on! One should sleep, play and enjoy life. Why hunt or fight? That is one intensive process! The extra layer of fat on us Yetis is evidence of this philosophy.' With this, Sago laughed, and the hall laughed with him. The building tension was released.

'But if the fight becomes unavoidable and someone else has started it, then fight like an elephant. Just swing your trunk here and there and shoo your enemy away. Let the other person know about your strength with a warning to not indulge in a fight. Fights and wars have never done well to anyone.'

Sago sighed deeply and continued, 'But we all know there are times when the fight becomes unavoidable. We face people who want to push us, bully us, and even go to the extent to destroy and eliminate us. Committing violence might not be correct, but tolerating violence is a sin! Even Arjuna[1] had to fight with his kinsmen, as there was no way out of fighting Adharma[2]! In such times, you must hunt like a tiger.

A tiger observes his prey without making the prey feel his presence. Tiger follows him for long paths. He observes, analyses, and chooses his target at its weakest. Then he waits, and just at the right time when his prey doesn't expect him, he ambushes the prey and finishes him off by giving his best.' Every word Sago said unfolded a different dimension in Dhriti's mind. Somewhere, she was realising what kind of mistake she was about to make... or had already made...

---

1 Arjuna was the protagonist of the Indian epic Mahabharata

2 Opposite of Dharma or non-righteous

'Likewise, you must start with observing your opponent, observe the behaviour and actions, even the minute ones. Understand and analyse the enemy with patience and try to find their weakness. Everyone has some weakness, even the great Achilles! Then, like a dexterous hunter, wait for the right time. When your opponent goes careless and doesn't expect any action from you, ambush them with full force and finish then and there.' A sudden shine of anger came to Sago's eyes with his rarely raised roaring volume. At the same time, his long hands moved stiffly, 'That's how you should fight!' with these words, Sago sighed all the energy he had gathered through the speech, and the hall was only echoing with his thunder. '... and this is how you culminate a successful batch!' The whole room laughed together.

Soon, everyone started to disperse, and the hall began to empty. There were three or four more people remaining, including Dhriti. She was sitting, her head hung down. She has realised that she was chosen to learn from the best, but her ego, stubbornness, and pride in being a rebel have made her lose this opportunity. The same three things were clinging her to the seat she was sitting on, not letting her go, talking to Sago, and asking for another chance. Instead, the three demons were trying to push her outside this hall, but somehow, Dhriti was sitting there fighting with them.

Suddenly, she realised someone was standing alongside her like the calm, serene mornings of the Himalayas. She could see the wavering white robe of this colossal Yeti figure. As she raised her head, repentance was dripping from her eyes. Sago saw her face, smiled, and said in his growling heavy voice, 'Tomorrow, 7 AM, my hall!'

ooo

16

LEARNINGS

Dhriti couldn't remember when she was so excited since she had come to the "Yeti World". She woke up at 5, got ready, and even revised the whole 6-month course. The Sago's speech has transformed Dhriti. Blinded by the aura of Gyatso, she couldn't expect anyone to be better than him. But Andre's question has reminded her who is the 'unbeatable' and yet humble to not sing about it. If she also wants to become unbeatable, Sago is the perfect person to guide her. Who knows, she would also find what she has lost in her journey to be the best.

With excitement in her eyes, Dhriti only reached Sago's hall at 6:50 AM, hoping to be the first one to greet him. But to her surprise, she found somebody else already conversing with the mentor. A tall girl clad in smart green formals with blond hair complimented her beauty. There was something in her that wouldn't let your attention sway away from her, even if thousands were sitting in a hall. Sago was so engrossed with her in the discussion that he couldn't notice that Dhriti was waiting for his glance at the hall door. Not being successful in getting the attention, she entered the hall while wishing Sago. To her surprise, Sago didn't respond to the morning wish, too. So, she went to the right to the front seat (as the front centre was occupied by this new girl) and deliberately put her learning device a little hard on the seat.

'Oh! Dhriti, good morning! When did you come?' Surprised, Sago asked.

'Around 5 minutes back. You were so engrossed that I didn't feel right to disturb you.' Replied Dhriti.

'Oh! Thanks a lot for your consideration. Galaxy has a good plan to support our education delivery system. It would be a system to enhance the focus of the students... Oh! Old soul me! I forgot to introduce you to Galaxy. Dhriti, meet Galaxy, Galaxy meet Dhriti.' Both of the girls had a formal handshake following Sago. 'You both are the best performers of your respective batches.' Listening to which eyes of both glared with pictures of each other.

'Crap! I was just revising the covered stuff, and this new bee has already taken the lead by "designing the system to enhance learning"! Come on, Dhriti, you need to step up your game.' The thought echoed relentlessly in Dhriti's mind. A day before, she would not have thought like this as she never wanted to "excel". But today, as she thought of giving her best and impressing Sago, the devil has sent this "Miss Future".

Eventually, in the session, Dhriti learned that Sago had taken only 5 teenagers under his wing. Others already knew this, as it was announced at the beginning of the training, and all four of them worked hard to land here. Dhriti would have known this if she had ever been interested in this training, especially under Sago. No other class interested her other than Gyatso's. Her focus in Sago's class was just to challenge whatever he said. The unconscious reason for this could be the wish to be at the top, as the quickest way to reach the top is to directly challenge the person at the top. This embarrassed her in class, but when did she care about it? Now, suddenly, she cared even about Sago's attention.

Dhriti also wondered what was special about her or her actions that landed her in the class. The other four had an interest in education. Some wanted to excel in research, others in training and technology concerning education, but Dhriti never thought of this. She never wanted to be part of this class. Then how come she landed with the best of the best students when others have landed at the place they wanted to?

The first session was small, and it finished with the revision of the 6-month course and the sharing of the future schedule and milestones. Students were given some videos to watch for the next class as homework, and the class dispersed. But Dhriti's mind was still hung on – why her? So, as everyone was leaving the class, Dhriti went close to Sago and waited for Galaxy to clear her doubts. She didn't want any company while she put her doubts down. As Galaxy left, Dhriti asked, 'May I ask you a question?'

Sago raised his eyes from his device and asked, 'Why are you here? Again?'

'You know what I mean…'

'Everyone has worked hard to be here, but have you just landed?'

'Yeah! Exactly!'

'I don't know!' Sago left a smile and started to leave the class.

'Sago Dada, come on! Please answer my question.' Dhriti kept pleading like a child but Sago kept walking as if she didn't exist.

'I don't know Dhriti. I don't have the answer to every question. And maybe this is not a question for me, but you… why are you here?' These words put a break on Dhriti's sprint and pushed her into the abyss of analysis and contemplation to answer the question – Why was she here?

ooo

17

GALAXY

Dhriti has been an achiever all her life, from the day she enrolled in the school. She has always been an ace, whether in academics, painting (which she left a long time ago), or even physical sports activity (she was a good swimmer). Although she never bragged about it, she has always been proud of this. Who would not be? This did not come as a gift to her; she had worked hard for it and had achieved it. Even after coming here, the pattern followed. Besides being the best person and the one to answer the most questions, she was the only one who dared to challenge Sago, not once but many times. All of these events and many more things kept forging the belief of being an achiever in herself till she met Galaxy.

It started on the first day of the internship only. From that day onwards, Galaxy was always one step ahead of Dhriti. Dhriti might think of doing something; Galaxy would have already done the same by then. Whether it was about completing the work, answering the questions, or taking new initiatives. There was not even one thing in which Dhriti was able to defeat Galaxy. There was a time when students could not forget Dhriti, but the new group hardly knew Dhriti.

Everyone wanted to be with Galaxy and used to go to her in case of any problem or needed guidance. Galaxy became Dhriti of this new class, but there was a difference. Despite being a shy girl, Dhriti was well-behaved with everyone, but Galaxy never saw Dhriti. She acted as if Dhriti didn't even exist. After all, Dhriti also didn't do anything yet that she would be a proven opponent.

Gradually, there came a time when she felt as if she was not there in the class at all. She became invisible, even for Sago! Dhriti has never experienced this kind of feeling before. Whether she would like it or not, she was always the focus of attention everywhere she went. Many others must have felt invisible because of her, but never her. Once you have been on top, it is not easy to see yourself there anymore, and here Galaxy was sweeping the floor with Dhriti.

Does this mean that Dhriti did not try? She did! She tried working harder, starting to be more attentive in class, and revising her notes, but every effort would wane. Even while Dhriti was trying to work hard, the maximum attention was on Galaxy, wondering how she must be doing the task. This could be the reason that, however hard she might have tried, she was hitting rock bottom again and again. This new girl was a class apart from her.

Ultimately, Dhriti was just left with two options – Let it go and don the mask of "I don't care!" again or pull up the socks and become the Dhriti of the school time she was, who worked hard as a bee with the passion of a butterfly. She chose the... first option. Her participation had already turned non-existent, but her presence in the class had also started to decrease. Whenever she joined the class, she joined late. Even when she was in the class, she never paid attention; at least, she tried to show it. She thought that this rebellious attitude would affect Sago and automatically, he would start paying attention to her, but that never happened. Sago was unmoved by her "new behaviour", and her rebellious attitude fell on deaf ears.

Now what? Even the last arrow of her quiver was wasted. It was the second time in her life she was feeling helpless. The first was just after the abduction of her father, and the second seems to be with the abduction of her authentic self. She couldn't figure out the next step. The blow was so hard that she started to be enslaved by her thoughts, and the thought whirlpools turned out to be her new home. The interaction with the group also went to almost zero. She used to be there with them but was still absent. There were no fights with Andre or leg-pulling of Salma; she just went numb. Salma and Andre both tried to figure it out but failed. Failure of egoistic people is always personal and often devastating.

A month dragged on like this only. Eventually, the day came for the announcement of the monthly assessment results. Galaxy outshined everyone, as expected, but another girl who was on top before gathered attention again. Dhriti didn't come last but failed! Dhriti flung the exams! In the training designed by Yetis, no human has failed in any of the classes. People didn't even know if there was a provision like that. Dhriti hadn't hit a low but was in an unfathomable abyss. She got clear instructions in the message received by the central coordinator that she could only stay in the batch if passed, or else she would be shifted to some other mentor.

The message was blinking on her device and Dhriti was numb. Tears were dropping from her eyes, but she was as cold as an iceberg. She didn't even realise that the session was over. Dhriti was just sitting on her seat, unmoved like a sky scrapper that had become dust due to a sudden Earthquake. They say that there is a place, just between life and death, where you cease to exist but still keep breathing, Dhriti must have been there. She came back to life due to the sound of a snap. It was Galaxy, standing right in front of Dhriti.

'I never knew it would be so easy.' Said Galaxy while adjusting her golden locks.

'What would be so easy?' Perplexed, Dhriti asked.

'To defy you! I have heard a lot about you – "Dhriti is so confident, Dhriti is so intelligent, Dhriti is Sago's favourite, Dhriti is this, Dhriti is that." People have exaggerated you. You were not that great. Even if I had sleepwalked the class, you never stood a chance. I didn't defy Dhriti, but I have destroyed you!

Sheer waste of time! Dhriti the star! Star my foot! Huh!' Galaxy rolled her eyes and went away.

It was hot, boiling lava put directly in the ears of Dhriti. Hearing what Dhriti has heard, anyone would have broken down then and there, but not Dhriti. This is not what her father has nurtured her to be. He didn't call her "raging bull" for no reason! When she was seven, she broke the teeth of the boy who had hit her best friend. This girl has hit the self-respect of the same girl! Whatever one may do, one should never make an elephant angry, and now she was mad angry.

OOO

18

THE TITANS

The next day was not that usual. Galaxy entered the class at 6:45, expecting it to be vacant, but it wasn't. Somebody was already sitting on the last central seat, Dhriti. 'Oh, poor Dhriti, you worked so hard to impress Sago by coming early to the class! I am proud of you!' Galaxy threw the sarcasm with a smirk. But that smirk just slipped away from Dhriti without making any impact. Gradually, everyone, including Sago, came to the class, and Dhriti kept sitting in the last row unmoved and still. The tiger was observing!

Today, Sago came in a different mood. His feet danced on some old rhythm with his fingers moving on the same. Whenever this had happened before, he had been in the mood of mischief and to test the students. Finally, with a twinkle of mischief in his eyes, he started speaking, 'It has been more than

7 months that we are studying education, human behaviour, psychology, etc., 6 months of the basic course and one month of training. So, I am going to ask you a question that is very simple yet very difficult. One who has focused sincerely would only be able to answer correctly. The question can assess your progress beyond any other tool.' Students patiently listened to him and were eager to answer the question. Answering this question would have meant impressing their favourite teacher. 'So, young blood, please tell me, what is education?' Sago rolled the dice of the question

Within a fraction of a second of the question being asked, a hand rose from the last bench. Sago smiled as if he expected this: 'Yes, Dhriti, please enlighten us!'

Everyone in the class turned and saw this 'new' person, who replied assertively, 'Education is the ability to differentiate between right and wrong!'

'Wow! The question was as simple as the answer. I love it, and you are correct!' Sago replied while clapping for Dhriti, and others followed him. The class later went into a critical and creative debate that was again aced by Dhriti.

That day was the milestone from where Dhriti's road took the turn of progress. "Hand-raised" started and kept on increasing, day by day. Her exploring questions started to disturb the topics again. She began to look happier again, with confidence gracing her face. Dhriti also started to talk to other students in the class, helping them wherever she could. Everyone was in love with this new Dhriti. Her group was also relaxed again, seeing the smile back on her face. But one person did not like even an ounce of it, Galaxy. With every risen hand of Dhriti, Galaxy's soul charred a little from the inside.

Any change is not easy, nor was this, not even for Dhriti. She has to change a lot, but thankfully, the change was not deliberate. Whenever the session was over, she would rush towards her room. Salma or whosoever might ask her to spend some time, she always had one answer – "Sorry, I need to study!" Initially, it was a shock to the friends, but gradually, it became a new pattern. A person who spent more time in the common-room than sessions was hardly found there anymore. Even Yua was surprised by her sudden change of schedule and behaviour. In the beginning, she felt that it was the result of a day's pressure, but it wasn't. Whether it was a day or a night, studies seemed to have become the new partner for Dhriti.

But Galaxy was a stubborn person herself, never an easy person to go down. She was not the one who would give up seeing the harsh waves, she was the one who would like to ride those waves! Gradually, the sessions looked more like Gladiator battles or the dual of Bhima[1] and Duryodhana[2] from Mahabharata. Galaxy would pick her heavy mace and answer the questions with her whole might. Still, in the next moment, Dhriti would not only save herself from this blow but would solve an unsolvable riddle like having a cake and would give a dhobi-pachhad to Galaxy. But throughout these duals, the lucky ones were the classmates, who were enjoying these mesmerizing matches without any tickets, and that too from the VIP seats. Everyone used to wait to see who would have the most brutal blow. Galaxy hit impeccably with great force, but the loud claps always came on Dhriti's passionate, out-of-the-box blows. The class became an arena for the Clash of the Titans. Sometimes, Sago just sat and meditated in the class, as the girls had already taken his discussion job. The class was learning by the sheer debate of the girls.

This new achievement acted as fuel for Dhriti. She started being happy, as she started being 'somebody' again in her vision. Dhriti had made a comeback, but something still irked her. She felt as if something was missing. She was winning, but the winner was not Dhriti! It was some other girl that she was turning into.

ooo

---

1 Elder brother of Arjuna from the Indian epic Mahabharata and a supporter of Arjuna. He fought with mace and was supposed to have the power of 10,000 elephants.

2 The antagonist of the Indian epic Mahabharata. He was at par with Bhima and fought with mace as his favourite weapon.

19

MEMORY LANE

A lot was going around for Dhriti – A new place, new people, new responsibilities, intense competition, rigorous classes and whatnot! As Sago could see her going active again, he added responsibilities to her. Now, he had two assistants, Galaxy and Dhriti. Assistants who would not see each other eye to eye. Dhriti was juggling so many tasks that she even forgot to have nutrition pills many times. But she never forgot one thing, to be one with the sun at the sunset every evening.

Sunsets were a little different in the Himalayas. One can't see the sun "setting" regularly, meeting the horizon. The sunset was very early, but that doesn't mean that nights came early, too. The light stayed even after the sun went behind the mountains. The reflection of the rays from the ice made it way different. It felt as if, even after setting, the sun used to fight with the mountains to return. Hence, there were long twilights!

Dhriti felt as if she had an old connection with this setting sun. Howsoever the day might have been, the setting sun used to fill her with peace and hope. It was a symbol of consistency. Whatever may happen, this event was bound to happen. Somehow, it forged her belief that if light can arrive even after sunset, then every problem should have a solution.

But more than anything, this setting sun was a time machine that used to take her down memory lane. She used to watch almost every sunset with her father. Whatever could be going on in the world, howsoever hectic life could have been yet, Dhairya ensured that he never missed a sunset with his moon, his daughter! He always attended the sunset, whether being physically present, through hologram conferencing or telepathically. It was their moment! The father-daughter moment! Especially after Dhriti's mother's demise, he always ensured he was there for her. Dhriti's mother was as courageous and an explorer as Dhriti. She was a space scientist and died in an accident while exploring another galaxy. Since that day, Dhairya has been Dhriti's mother, father, joker, teacher, or whatever she wanted him to be until the robots came and took them away. Dhriti didn't only lose her father then, she lost everything!

Dhriti still remembered it clearly, as if it happened yesterday. It was 10 PM or so at night. She was designing her science project of building a spacecraft hologram modal. Dhriti always had a keen interest in space physics. It could be something she would have inherited from her mother. Joining different parts she designed from the hologram designer, she was keenly building the spacecraft. The person who built the closest to the actual spacecraft would make the trip to the moon. Her father was challenging her with possible problem questions regarding the project, 'So miss aero-physicist, I can see that you can launch your mini ship, but how will you make it land?'

Suddenly, there was a knock on the door. Dhairya stood up to answer the door. He can't see the person on the door sitting in his room as he used to before. Robots have taken away all those "privileges". He opened the door and found two robots waiting. Before he could think anything else, he was made unconscious. 5 minutes later, Dhriti, who was lost in the project, asked a question to her father. After not getting the answer, she realised her father hadn't returned. Dhriti went to check the door, but the door was open, and he was nowhere. She thought he might have gone to a nearby place, but later, she learned what actually happened with her father as the same thing had happened to other parents too. All of them have been abducted.

Since that day, there was not a moment when she did not regret opening the door that day. Innumerous times, she tried changing that situation. 'I should have answered the door... I could have gone with him... I could have saved him...' Many thoughts came to her head, but none were of any use. Just like a soldier who has lost the battle, she tried to change the outcome by fighting it again and again in her mind, but the war was already lost! She cried for the whole week. The week felt like centuries. No food, neither water, only regrets and guilt. The only thing she had in life was taken away from her. How could she live?

Then, one day, her prayers were answered. Again rang the doorbell, and she ran like an uncontrolled blizzard slipping on the path of hope. But as she reached the door and was about to open it, her mind started working, and she doubted that it could be robots again who had come to abduct her this time. So, she picked an iron rod and started approaching the gate; it was the best option available for self-defence. While getting ready, she had already beaten and broken those robots before opening the door in her imagination. But she was shocked as she opened the door. It was her father who was waiting there for her. Finally, fate was being kind to her.

She just hugged him and kept crying. She tried saying many things and asked many questions, but mixed with the tears and hiccups, only Dhairya could have understood that, or did he? After a moment, she realised it was only she who hugged her father; he did not reciprocate the hug. She felt as if she was hugging a mannequin of flesh and bones. This was very awkward and unexpected. As she watched her father's face, it had no expression and only stared at the wall opposite him. 'Leave me, girl. I need to work,' he said in a straight, non-expressive voice. He pushed Dhriti away and went straight inside.

This was even a bigger shock, beyond any understanding of Dhriti. 'How was that even possible?' But the "possible" had already started working in the house. Was the person who entered the house her father, or did a robot replace him? Dhriti noticed the mark over Dhairya's bald head, which suggested some surgery; the robots didn't bother to remove the mark. They could have wanted to convey some message to the children, and it seems the message of fear and cruelty was conveyed aptly. Dhriti ran some tests, and all the conclusions were that the person was her father. But how? It felt as if this new person never knew Dhriti. He was always busy at work like a robot and never talked or responded to her. 'Did he have a brainwash?' There were many questions, and she had to find the answers.

She kept trying to make him remember the great relationship they had nurtured by sharing different old holographic photographs and retelling the stories of their different memories, but Dhairya couldn't remember anything. Not even a single fold came upon his face, and there was not even a tingle in his eyes when he saw those objects. Every day, Dhriti would try something new in the hope of him remembering her through that. In the hope of this object getting transformed into a switch to bring the love back, but nothing changed.

She tried consulting others-doctors, scientists, other elders-and made every possible connection, but every road hit a dead end. After all, to whom she could consult, like her father, every other adult on the planet had lost their emotions, and there was no way they could return. It was a mass raid by robots on every adult human. They have stolen the emotions from adult humans and every happiness from Dhriti's life... with just one doorbell.

Since then, Dhriti has never done two things: She has never shut the door of her room and has never studied Astrophysics.

ooo

20

WAY OUT

Like any other evening, Dhriti was lost in the same loop of memories when suddenly Salma snapped in front of her face, 'Come back, madam!' Dhriti was taken back to the present with the snap. 'I often doubt you can see something else in this setting sun. Something that you passionately desire. The boy of your dreams! The tall... fair... handsome... long-haired... Yeti!'

'You scoundrel!' The chase started, which ended with Salma being caught and getting never-ending tickles from Dhriti. After apologising hundreds of times and ultimately being forgiven by Dhriti, both friends joined the regular chit-chat. But Dhriti was still lost, and tension was dancing on her face!

'Are you fine?' Salma asked as she was again about to lose Dhriti in some invisible sunset.

'Nah! I am not!' Dhriti replied after a little bit of thinking.

'What happened, again thinking about stars and "Galaxies"?' Salma pulled Dhriti's leg.

'I didn't know you could read minds, miss psycho!' Dhriti replied to Salma in the same tone but then sighed deeply and continued, 'I don't know what kind of problem she has with me! Since day one, she has been hounding me… trying to "devastate me", but I don't know why! What harm have I caused her?'

'Hmmm, Dhriti, do you know the smallest way to solve a problem?' Salma asked with a smile on her face.

'Now, you will also talk like Sago? As if this was the only thing missing in my life!' Dhriti replied in disappointment.

'Facing it head-on. Isn't it? But we never think about it. We keep planning and strategising, but sometimes, going straightaway to solve the problem is the best way. Right? Why don't you ask the question to its source itself? Things can't get worse than they already are…' Salma suggested.

'Yeah! You are right… I should communicate with her.' Dhriti replied while thinking.

'And with this deep "wisdomful" answer, Salma got promoted to "Salma Dada!"' Salma started aping Sago, using her long hair as the beard and both of the friends were in splits in no seconds.

21

CEASE-FIRE

The fifth month of the internship had arrived. Everything was going as usual: experiential learning facilitated by Sago, regular assignments and challenges, and duels between Galaxy and Dhriti—a duel enjoyed by everyone, including Sago. Although the competition was always of almost equal scale, and in recent times, Dhriti's wins were in the majority, she was still unhappy.

This was not Dhriti. She never gave dirt about such competition. She always did whatever she felt like, in the ways she wanted to, with just the thought of making it better. The process in itself was a motivation for her. She never considered competition a great choice; instead, she tried to help others improve their work. So, while completing the regular tasks, Salma's advice hovered over her head consistently.

She was trying her best to find the right time to talk to Galaxy, but somehow, it was slipping away.

'Dhriti, are you with us?' Sago asked for the second time. Sago called Dhriti's name as he wanted to ask her to come to the front of the class, and thankfully, Dhriti heard it in the second time.

'So, young-bloods, as you know, the internship is about to end, and your final assignment would be the project. Here, we have a bowl through which you will choose the topic of your project. You will be building the project in pairs. The person called to the front will be free to choose his/her partner. A person who would be left alone at last will get me as the "penalty partner", as I am the worst partner. I make my partners work the most!' Sago laughed, and everyone smiled with him. 'So, Dhriti, I have not invited you to begin anything in this internship until now. Hence, you start this process!' announced Sago.

A transparent bowl lay in front of Dhriti. There were many ways of doing this exercise, like random selection through a machine, comparing 'students' profiles, and matching them according to their strengths and weaknesses, but Sago always believed in the old methods. As he often said, the "feel" in the classic methods made them more magical! Dhriti put her hand confidently into the bowl, picked out a chit, and read it aloud. 'Our Education!'

'Yes! So now, you need to create your model of education. Whom would you like to choose as your partner?' Sago asked with curiosity. All the eyes in the room were focused on Dhriti's choice and nervousness about whether they would be part of it. But Dhriti put everyone in shock with her announcement, 'Galaxy!'

What? How was that possible? Why would Dhriti do this? Choosing her nemesis for the most important project of the training? Everyone in the room had a jaw drop, but Sago. He had a triumphant smile on his face. As if he knew everything - Why did Dhriti choose Galaxy? What did she have in her mind? And what was about to happen next? Sago might have known everything, but no one else, not even Dhriti.

Finally, the class ended with everyone having perplexed faces. Rather than their project with their respective partners, everyone was eager to see the result of this association in which two poles were about to meet. Will it be the end of the world or the beginning of a new one? As soon as everyone dispersed after the class, Galaxy almost jumped on Dhriti like a hungry lioness, 'What's this trickery?'

Surprisingly enough, Dhriti replied with a smile. As if she knew in advance that this would happen, 'What do you mean? What trickery?'

Fuming, Galaxy replied, 'You have a fair idea that we don't see each other eye to eye, then how dare you choose me as a partner? You must have plans to make me look down!'

'Galaxy, I have never had any problem with you. It was only you who had the problem. I honestly consider you the best in our class, so I wanted to work with you so that I, too, can get good grades...' Dhriti replied with a smile.

Galaxy was not prepared for such a calm, composed, and appreciative reply. She was dumbstruck. There was no comeback for what Dhriti had said. There could be a lot of what she wanted to say, but none of that would be the reply to what Dhriti had said to her. There is no other way to respond to appreciation rather than gratitude or appreciation, but how could Galaxy thank her opponent?

'I don't know your plan yet, but I am not scared of you either. I am not lesser than you anyhow. I accept your this challenge, and I will see you!' Saying this, Galaxy left the room, stomping her feet.

'Sure, but see me at 8 in the evening today. We will discuss the project!' Dhriti yelled high so that the voice landed on the ears of Galaxy.

For the whole time, from 3 to 8 PM, Galaxy was just trying to figure out, 'Why!" Why does Dhriti want to work with her? Is there a definite motif, or is it just another way to disturb her?' There were many questions, but none had the answers. Whatever the reason, Dhriti definitely shocked Galaxy with this action. Galaxy could not expect this even in the wildest of her dreams. What should she do now? Should she give up on this challenge? Never! With a lack of options, Galaxy ultimately decided to face Dhriti confidently and not reveal to Dhriti that she was clueless about her next move. Meanwhile, she will figure out Dhriti's objective. It was the internship's last phase, and she didn't want to slip on this.

As planned, Dhriti and Galaxy met at 8 PM in the common hall. Only a few people were in the common hall then, so it was mainly them. The talk started to discuss the idea. 'So, Galaxy, what do you think we should work on? The content or the method? Should we suggest some new technology to make the process more efficient?' Dhriti initiated the discussion curiously.

'Have you lost it, Dhriti? Their technology is so superior to ours! How can we even think of surpassing that?' Galaxy rejected the idea bluntly.

'Hmm, you are correct. It might be a little difficult. So, what do you think?' Dhriti asked, and like this, the conversation continued for more than an hour and kept hitting dead ends. This one hour felt like ages passing by. For the whole of the time, both of them kept rejecting each other's thoughts and ideas. They were trying hard from the outside, but something that had grown inside needed resolving first. It felt like a catch-22 situation, and even the brains soon gave up.

'Should we take a break, Galaxy? We can't go ahead like this…' Asked Dhriti with a sigh.

"I already knew this Dhriti. We are never supposed to work together. We can't!" Galaxy replied, who had already piled on to her frustration, and now it has hit the brink. 'Why did you even think of this idea? Be honest and tell!'

'Because I could not understand why you hated me so much! I have never done anything bad to you… rather, I adore your hard work. I don't want to be your enemy, Galaxy. We both are intelligent and together…'

'No, Dhriti. A girl like you would never work with a girl like me! We can't ever work together!' Galaxy replied assertively.

Dhriti asked with concern, 'But why? And what do you mean by "my type" of girl? Do you even know me?'

'I already know you! I know girls like you who are gifted and talented.' Spoke Galaxy while concentrating on nowhere, as if she was seeing something… someone… 'People like you might show they are with people like me, but they are never. You guys always take advantage of us, and when we have our guards down at the right time, you ditch us!" Galaxy replied intensely, and then there was a pin-drop silence between them. Dhriti broke the silence with a rub on the Galaxy's shoulder and said in a low voice, 'Hey! What had happened to you?'

Galaxy went a step ahead, leaving Dhriti's touch. 'Nothing that must bother you! I will go to Sago Dada tomorrow and ask him to change this group. Goodbye!' said Galaxy, who was about to storm out of the hall.

'And what do you think? Sago Dada will follow your will? Didn't you see the broad smile on his face as I chose you as my partner? He wants to see things beyond possibility, things like us working together. Although you know this, still let me tell you. He will give you 2 options, either continue with me or fail the internship. Are you ready to fail?' Dhriti never wanted to do this, but ultimately, she pressured Galaxy to open her up. That was the last resort.

Dhriti's words stopped the storming out Galaxy. She froze, hearing the truth in Dhriti's words. She didn't want to work with Dhriti, but the last thing she wanted was to fail the internship. Dhriti has played an ace! '

'Galaxy, caldera lake can't be built unless the lava inside the volcano is put out', said Dhriti. She again approached Galaxy from behind and said with utmost empathy, 'Please tell me, what happened? I can't withstand your envy.'

'It is not something that "had happened"; it has been happening, Dhriti." Galaxy's voice started to break, so she paused, took a seat, and continued. 'I was the daughter of an intelligent couple; both were world-renowned scientists who always stayed occupied with the work of their "World Addressals". Both were prodigy children, the gifted ones who had been talented since birth, but I was not. I was just a regular child who always performed less than her parents' expectations. I tried hard… very hard… but the mountain of expectations was way higher than my calibre. They must have seen the failure they had created. With disappointment in me, they brought home a sister, a child that they deserved.

She was 5 years old and must be the cutest and most adorable thing I ever saw. We loved each other even more than real siblings. As my parents never had time, I was the one who nurtured her. She also adored me so much that she never used to leave me unless our parents asked her to. I was so happy, as finally, I had someone with whom I could talk to. I used to share everything with her – thoughts, feelings, ideas, belongings, everything! I was good with ideas, and she was good at developing them. We were a complementary team. But one day, I got to know that she shared all of those ideas with our parents as hers. There was no reason that they would doubt her. Soon, she also joined the "prodigy club", and I was left alone.' There was silence between the Dhriti and Galaxy, which was filled with sobbing.

'I am sorry that this happened to you, Galaxy. I didn't know you were going through so much.' Said Dhriti while rubbing Galaxy's shoulder as she was sobbing.

Galaxy was still watching her past life pass once again in front of her, and she continued. 'It was not all Dhriti. I am not so weak that I would cry over a childhood memory till today.' Galaxy sighed and continued, 'I looked way more mature than my age, and accidentally, robots took me away, perceiving me as an adult. They did something to my brain that somehow enhanced it. They experimented on me and instantly, I became intelligent by folds, a "natural one", as my parents wanted. They were about to take emotions out of me, but in the middle of the process, they got to know that I was not an adult, and as a result, they sent me back. I felt that I would finally be accepted by my parents, but by the time I arrived, they had already lost their emotions. Although, I wonder if they ever had! I was left alone again.

Ultimately, I came here for another start and saw Sago Dada. I saw a father figure in him that I never had in life. This time, I didn't want to make any mistakes; life gave me a second chance. This time, I was exceptional, too; the only front over which I lagged before. Soon, with my enhanced intelligence, I became his favourite, but then the batches were mixed, and you came in. I already knew how much he liked you. After all, after decades, there came someone who could challenge him and...'

'You saw your younger sister in me and got scared...' Dhriti added. Listening to this, Galaxy nodded in acceptance, and Dhriti continued, 'And that's why you started doing things to me, what your younger sister did to you!' Hearing this, Galaxy's eyes stretched in shock. She could never see what she was doing and why she was doing it. All of a sudden, the last 5 months rolled in front of her eyes like a movie roll, a movie in which she has been a villain. A villain she has been running from.

Galaxy got filled with sudden guilt!

'Galaxy, if you could realise, I am just you from some years back. Struggling to compete with you and trying my level best for the same. I am sorry for whatever happened to you, but I am just a regular teenager... A teenager whom you can trust.

If you still don't, you can get all the grades for this project. Earning a friend is more important for me than getting some stupid grades!' Hearing this, Galaxy caressed the hand of Dhriti, which was already on her shoulder, and said the three most beautiful words repeatedly: 'I am sorry!'

ooo

22

LEVEL UP!

Next week, the presentation by DG (Dhriti – Galaxy group, Galaxy only suggested putting Dhriti's name first) group was beyond the limit of expression. The presentation seemed to be like a firework. Great idea with impeccable presentational skills.The presentation's theme was "Every Child Has a Universe Within". The project advocated that every child has the potential to change this universe, and every child should be motivated to explore within. It also talked about different methods that can be implemented to explore the potential of various kinds of children – methodologically and technologically.

The final project presentation happened in the main hall, and the thunderous applause must have made the Himalayas feel a little weak inside.

Ultimately, it was the last week of the training, and everyone was just going on the class observation of younger students with Sago. It was time to check the understanding they had built over time and the application aspect of learning. Sago felt this was the right time to test Dhriti in the boiling waters. So, as he met her in the morning to plan the day, his vocabulary was a little different. His instructions had a lot of 'you' than 'us', like, 'You will go to the class, and you will have a session on anything you want to have.' Dhriti could gauge this change and rightfully asked with apprehension, 'Sago Dada, are you making any mistake today? I mean... you are using 'you' rather than 'us' today...'

Sago saw Dhriti's confused face and smiled, 'It is not a mistake, Dhriti. Today is your day; you will take the class alone today.'

The carpet was pulled from under Dhriti's feet. She felt the nightmare in which the exam was taken a week before as the surprise and everyone failing had come to life. 'But why... How... wasn't it supposed to happen...?' Dhriti fired a list of questions on Sago. But Sago replied unmoved, 'You are ready, Dhriti. You don't need another week. Just believe in yourself and flow like a river, no extra pressure. All the best!'

Sago passed his trademark warm smile and moved on, unbothered.

Dhriti was left in a pool of doubts. She knew that this day would come, but just like we all know that, death is going to come. But what if someone tells you that you are about to die now? Aren't you going to shit in your pants? Similar was the condition with Dhriti. She always thought that Sago would share this with her in advance and she would have time to prepare, but the next moment, she was standing in front of the class of 7-year-olds.

'Why do we need to follow these Yeti ways of learning? It was so comfortable learning at our houses in the past. Why do we need these ancient classes again?' Dhriti started talking to herself as if it was going to help her. The human world had everything recorded, and human children were being taught by robots online through hologram conference-based classes. However, physical classes were necessary for humans to develop a feeling of community. It was also part of Yeti's way of learning. They believed that a person doesn't only learn from the teacher but from the whole learning environment; a person not only learns the subject but way more than that in a class. So, when in Rome, act like Romans!

Dhriti was stuck between the devil and the deep sea. Just the thought of entering the class was giving her jolts. She imagined how these little devils were about to bully her once she was there unprepared. At the same time, she could not avoid the class; if she did, she would break Sago's trust. Finally, she thought of testing the waters before entering them, and she peeped through the door gap.

Oh, dear god! It was not the class. It was a circus with different kinds of animals performing together with no synchronisation. Someone was jumping on the seat for no reason, somebody was in the mood of singing, a group was playing some random game that they had made instantly, and there was also a kid sobbing in a corner. Dhriti just closed her eyes, prayed to the god, took a deep breath, and banged into the door—the way she generally took any risk in life!

As she stepped inside the class, a collective cheer welcomed her. 'Good morning, *didi*[1]!'

'Good morning, everyone!' Dhriti tried her best to revert the cheer. Even the children were a little confused after her entry, as today, it was not followed

---

1 Respectful word for the elder sister in many Indian languages

by Sago Dada and his growling yet affectionate voice.

'Didi, Sago Dada hasn't come today?' A girl with 2 ponies asked, and others joined her curiosity.

'Aaaaa, no! It's only me.' After saying this, Dhriti could read the disappointment rising on the children's faces. Sensing this, her brain started to go into alarm mode: 'What should I do now? Maybe I should start teaching them by taking their questions.'

Brimming with happiness and spilling some nervousness, Dhriti asked the students, 'As we know that Dada is not here, we will study whatever you want to. So, are there any questions you wanted to ask but never asked?'

Students got perplexed as this was happening for the first time with them. Dhriti was trying to replicate how Sago taught them, but the way of teaching young kids and teenagers is not the same. The children couldn't figure out what they wanted to ask, although there had been many questions they wanted to ask in the past. Then young Santiago raised his hand and asked, 'Didi, what is sex?'

Oops! Dhriti knew that she had asked for bullets, but she didn't expect to get the atomic bomb in the first go only. She had opened Pandora's Box, and she could never be prepared for what was about to follow:

"Didi, why is Himalaya so high?"

"Didi, why are we made different from Yetis?"

"Didi, how does the air blow?"

"Didi, why can't we fly like birds?"

"Didi, is Mars Man real?"

Dhriti was attacked from almost every side of the Himalayas, and she was about to go unconscious. Instantly, Sago's growling voice echoed in her head, "If there is no fun, then one can't learn!"

Dhriti yelled at her loudest, 'Waiiiiiiiiiiiiiiit!" which was enough to make the room go silent. "Who would like to play a game?'

The answer obviously landed in an even louder voice, 'WE!'

Then, all together, a new flow came to the class. One game after the other, something based on science, something on mathematics or something on language. Children were running, jumping, pushing, pulling, dancing, acting and whatnot! The only subjects that seemed to be being taught were fun and laughter. Even Dhriti couldn't realise when the 4 hours got over, she was supposed to leave this class.

'OK, children, see you tomorrow!' Dhriti bid adieu, but multiple hands were raised in response. With a sceptical tone, she asked, 'Now what?'

'Best class ever didi!' The class yelled back.

Galloping with happiness, Dhriti opened the gate of the class and found Sago standing there.

'You? When did you come here?' Asked surprised Dhriti.

'I was always here!' replied Sago with a smile.

Dhriti just ran and hugged him after that, or maybe the seven-year-old in her did that.

ooo

23

DHRITI VS DHRITI

'Dhriti di, why couldn't we defy robots?' asked 10-year-old Oliver after raising his hands.

'What do you think Oliver?' Dhriti asked in return.

'I think... because they were made of metals and were way stronger than us.' Perplexed, Oliver replied while scratching his red head. He generally tried to answer first, even if he did not know the answer.

'Ha ha, yes! This could be one of the reasons. What about others? What do you think?' With this, Dhriti opened the floor for the whole class. She was teaching for six months, and by now, she has almost become a pro. This doesn't mean she doesn't get nervous in class, but she handles it anyhow. Who can ever be one hundred per cent ready for any job?

'I think they are way more intelligent than us,' Little Chloe replied in her British accent while adjusting her spectacles. Chloe was the only second person on campus who wore spectacles. The glasses didn't have any power, but they were her mother's, hence oversized and often needed adjustment.

'No! They must have attacked with a surprise!' Milani countered the argument. Milani was another intelligent kid in the class who was good at finding solutions. With Milani's answer, the class went into another debate. Debates were common and crucial in Dhriti's class. Everyone was supposed to put their point of view in the class, and others had the freedom to counter it. There was no absolute right or wrong in this class.

'Actually, you all are correct. We were not ready for it and were too dependent on robots. Somewhere in our endeavour to win the solar system, we got very egoistic and maybe our ego blinded us. It was also our failure to mobilize our people in that short time and...'

Dhriti was cut by Yua instantly, 'But why not now?' Yes! Yua was the roommate of Dhriti and was now also the student of Dhriti.

'What do you mean, Yua? What not now?' confused Dhriti asked back.

'Why can't we defy them now? Now we are organised, we are aware of their and our weakness. We have better technology of Yetis, so why shouldn't we attack and get what was ours back?' Yua asked in her usual angry tone.

'No, this is not possible. We all are so young and so low in number that we can't endanger our existence. Do you know what they will do to us if they catch us? They will suck our brains and will make us logical robot-like our parents. We can't afford to lose what we have in the blind hope of having what we don't. This is too precious!' This thought instantly came to Dhriti's mind, but patiently, she let it pass and didn't share it with the class. With time, she has learned the wisdom to hold her thoughts and share them at the right moment. Anyway, teaching was not about telling but asking the right question. Instead, she asked, 'What do you think, Yua?'

Yua replied fumingly, 'Because you adults will never let us, you and the Yetis. Yetis have pacified you all. You have lost the battle and have accepted it, too. But we won't, we won't ever!'

The words were said so strongly that they pushed Dhriti into something she was trying to run away from, the old Dhriti!

Dhriti was now part of the governing body of humans, which was like Yetis' governing body. She added many responsibilities to her belt in the past 6 months. Galaxy and she were handling the education & training wing of humans under the guidance of Sago. From planning to implementation, both of them designed and monitored everything. Every evening, one meeting of the education and training team took place. Every week, the governing council was supposed to meet. She also has to give time to her new family and her friends. All of a sudden, this generation has to become mature enough to take care of their people.

Either she got so occupied with herself or got so comforted in this new world that she forgot the old Dhriti—the Dhriti who was a rebel and would not accept anything so easily. The Dhriti who wanted to be a disciple of Guru Gyatso, to get trained in fighting and eventually take vengeance from the "tin boxes". Where did that Dhriti go?

After a long time, today, she met the same Dhriti again, from the other side of the seat, speaking from the mouth of Yua. Every other face in the class might not have rebelled like Yua, but even they wanted to speak the same voice—a voice that old Dhriti used to have. But what about the new Dhriti? What did she want? To be settled in the mountains like these fury yogis?

Adulting had a cost. It had taken Dhriti away from Dhriti. The same old Dhriti stood in front of the new Dhriti, asking some questions—questions that this new Dhriti had forgotten—questions that this new Dhriti could not answer—questions that she needed to answer...

ooo

24

ON YOUR OWN

Dhriti was again standing in the middle of a storm. All she had were questions hovering over her like vultures, starving for answers, and she didn't have any answer, especially to the question of existence. Why was she doing what she was doing? Has she forgotten why did she join Sago? What about all the vengeance that she wanted to have? Has she also become just another "mature" person? How could she forget her father and what the tin monsters have done to him and her? She was standing stunned, with not even a muscle moving. She was numb. She was almost in sleep paralysis, but she was not sleeping.

Questions are a tricky part of life, but when they start to question your existence, they can be fatal!

Moving like a zombie through the corridor, Dhriti stopped suddenly, as if she had found Thor, who could save her from this storm. It was the hall of Sago. Without wasting a second, she just bumped into the hall where Sago was facilitating a class of younger students. Dhriti entered the hall and froze after taking two or three steps. Sago had never seen her like this before; her hairs were scattered, her eyes were red, and her face seemed to be dried with prolonged crying. Sago immediately turned back to his students and said, 'Dispersed! We will meet tomorrow at the same time.' The class dispersed with murmurs, leaving only Dhriti and Sago in the room. Sago immediately offered Dhriti water, but Dhriti instantly cried aloud, 'Why?'

'Bachcha, you seem to be very disturbed. Please drink the water first...' Sago tried to console Dhriti, but Dhriti stepped back. 'No! Not this time. I am disturbed, and I want to stay disturbed. Why have you made me "Settled", Dada? Why? You know what I wanted, but you still took me away from that. Why?' Dhriti was crying like anything while speaking.

'Dhriti, you are not in the right state...' Sago tried again, but Dhriti was not ready to hear anything today.

'No! I am in the right state today only, and I want answers. No more stories! No more divergence!' Dhriti continued with tears dropping from her cheeks. It was getting difficult for her to talk in between tears and hiccups.

'What kind of answers, bachcha? When haven't I answered you?' Sago replied with concern. He knew that Dhriti was disturbed and needed to be calmed down first, but she was not letting it.

'When are we starting the war against robots?' Dhriti asked while wiping her tears.

'Don't you know the answer to this question already, Dhriti?' Asked Sago in his usual style.

'But I want the answer from you!' Dhriti replied loudly.

'Yetis will never have war with robots, Dhriti...' Sago was cut by Dhriti in the middle only, 'But why Dada? Don't you have all the resources for the war? Isn't it your responsibility to have this war to save the universe? Isn't it your responsibility as our guardians to fight with us?' Dhriti asked while holding Sago's massive furry hand.

'It is Dhriti. We are preserving the universe. We are standing with all of you but in our way.' Dhriti turned away with these words, but Sago continued, 'It is not our nature! You can't use a shield like a sword! We are peace-builders, not war seekers. You need to understand us before having any expectations from us. Illogical expectations only hurt. We will support you in every right action, but the action has to come from you...'

Dhriti again cut Sago in between and angrily asked, 'What should we do? Keep sitting like this in the Himalayas until we become peace seekers like you?'

'This is one way of living life, but you need not choose this. You have to decide your path.' Sago tried to smile a little at this.

'Come on, Sago! Wouldn't you have gotten into war if robots had done this to you?'

Sago again replied calmly, 'Have robots done this to "us"?' After a pause, he continued, 'Dhriti, we don't say that you should not fight, but it is your war. We are here to support you in every way, but we can't lead it.'

Dhriti stared at Sago for 10 seconds and then left the hall like a typhoon breaking the walls of the dams.

OOO

25

NEXT-GEN!

The universe is vast and diverse, but some common truths or rules can still be discovered. Two such universal rules that can be traced anywhere are: the new generation will always conflict with just one generation before, and the new generation will be filled with hope, energy, and idealism. Things like fear and despair don't make sense to the young generation. They are filled with wonders and ideas and often feel that the last generation is useless (or at least they are better than them). They want to experiment and explore. Their fuel is hope, and their aircraft is imagination. The world is either great or can be great, if we see from their eyes. But the generation older than them is loathed with enough experience to be pessimistic about things, to be suspicious if things are going fine, to expect a wrong thing to happen, or in their words, to be "real". After all, once bitten, twice shy! But the young ones are not!

So, whatever was going on between Yua and Dhriti was very natural. The same Yua, who had found comfort in Dhriti as an older sister, started being away from her. Reason? Dhriti had become her class teacher. So, unknowingly, the two spaces began mingling. It was difficult for Dhriti to differentiate between home and school; for her, it was only Yua, her younger sister! How does that matter if she asked her to complete the homework first in the room or shared some examples from the room with the class in front of Yua's friends? But to Yua, it mattered most! She was already an introverted girl, but now she camouflaged in class. She couldn't afford to take the chance to make single eye contact with Dhriti and spill some personal information in the class, for which she would be teased later.

Yua was on an overdose of Dhriti, which could be a significant reason for the growing friction in their relationship. Yua was also about to become a tween, and the rebellious attitude comes as a "surprise gift" with that age. Dhriti was attempting to "improve" Yua's every action. Consequently, Yua's lips were sealed with a constant line: "You don't understand me!" This feeling shot up after the last class.

'So, what do you guys think?' Yua asked other students as Dhriti left the class.

'Regarding what?' Oliver asked with suspicion while adjusting his pants. He always wore long pants in the hope of gaining height.

'Regarding the way to defeat robots!' Yua replied aggressively yet in a suppressed voice. 'Our grown-ups are never going to find the solution for this problem. Only we have to find it! They all have gone old like Yetis!'

'I think Dhriti di was right…' Yua's burning gaze didn't let Chloe, the teacher's pet, complete the sentence. Chloe adjusted her spectacles to hide her embarrassment, and before the situation could have developed, Milani asked, 'Aren't we a little young to think this?'

'No! We are not eight anymore!' Oliver supported the argument of Yua. The argument further got support from everyone else.

'Hey! Maybe we should invent a new weapon to defy them. What do you say?' Gaurav, a passionate artist who kept designing new things in his imagination, said excitedly.

'That will take time…' Yua replied, contemplating the situation.

'I think we all can transform ourselves to look like robots. Then join their army and attack them by surprise!' Milani added to the brainstorming.

'Dumbo! We already look like them. The only difference is that all of them look like human adults, and we don't.' Oliver replied to Milani.

The discussion continued for hours, and many ideas were showered, but almost each one was rejected. The rejection hammer was in the hands of Yua and Oliver, who used it for every idea. Oliver already felt like a judge and started rejecting ideas as they were put by anyone, "No! Not possible." He could have made a song with these lyrics if Yua had not scolded him for "acting like adults". But even after not reaching any solution, everyone enjoyed this exercise. Discussing a big thing like adults was fun, irrespective of the outcome. But eventually, like grown-ups, the frustration started to rise. It was first expressed by Oliver, who yelled at everyone like their commandant, 'Come on guys! Let us listen to each other first. Otherwise, we will discuss this on a telepathy call. You all are so indisciplined and uncreative. Are you really the kids who are going to defy robots?'

Suddenly, Yua jumped with excitement, 'Oscar, TELE!'

'Ya! Telepathy!' Oscar felt proud that the real leader appreciated his idea without understanding her hint.

'Not telepathy, idiot! TELEPORTATION!' With these words of Yua, a smile came on everyone's face. They have finally cracked the code. It was their "eureka moment", and they really wanted to dance like Archimedes but avoided it due to the risk of getting caught by grown-ups. Instantly, the group made the huddle, and the plan started to take shape. Everyone was told with strict warnings from Oliver that this should not go out to adults or Yetis. Otherwise, he will personally look into the matter!

OOO

26

THE IDEA

Dhriti was sitting in her room, feeling betrayed by Sago. She needed and expected his support at this time. After all, he was supposed to be her mentor and guide! But expectations are like the white clouds that don't answer the hopes of rain. She felt cheated, as if all the trust she invested in Sago was flushed away with just one no from him. But deep down, even before asking, she knew Sago would never agree. He was a Yeti of principals. He would never go against values. These were amongst the many things that made him special, too. But right now, it didn't help Dhriti to not feel lonely. Anyway, what kind of relationship relationship flourishes without expectations? She has come to the same crossroads she was at one year before, with no direction to go ahead… lost… lonely…

While Dhriti was drowning in this trench of lost trust, suddenly, Andre came to her room holding his head. His eyes, along with his bright white face, have turned red with pain.

'Andre! What happened to you?' Dhriti asked in a tense tone.

'Ah! The nerve pain, Dhriti! It's back!' Said Andre with pain. Andre had nerve pain in his head when he arrived at the Yeti's world. This pain was so unbearable that Andre even used to get unconscious with it. But the advanced medical sciences of Yetis, based on nature, treated Andre. The pain vanished. One of the major conditions for the treatment was to bathe with cold water regularly. Initially, it was tough, but eventually, Andre made peace with it. But he accidentally had a warm water bath today, and consequently, the pain returned.

'Oh! Come inside and rest here. Have you taken the painkillers?' Dhriti asked. 'Oh! I forgot you don't take painkillers!'

'Yeti Vaidya[1] told me I will be fine in one hour. But I have a class... can you...' Andre managed to speak this much only while lying on Dhriti's bed. Every word hit him hard in this situation as he tried to talk.

'Yeah! Don't worry!' Dhriti started to get ready for the class.

---

1 A word for doctors used in many Indian languages including Sanskrit

'But it is sunset...' It was evident that Andre couldn't speak.

'It is OK, Andre! The world won't come to an end if I don't see the sunset one evening.' Dhriti had never missed a single sunset since the day she had come to this place. It was not merely a sunset but more like the meeting time for her with her father. But it was an emergency, and she could bend her rule for one day. There was no other option.

While going through the module to be taught, she realised one more thing she had not done in ages, studying physics! It was a huge pain point for Dhriti. It used to trigger painful memories of how she lost her mother because of Space & physics and how much she suffered because of that. She promised herself that she would never study physics, but what would she do now? Every teenager was supposed to teach something to students, and Andre taught them physics. Realising the possible impact of teaching physics, Dhriti turned to Andre to ask if anyone else could teach the subject. Still, she couldn't say anything after watching Andre crying in pain.

So, somehow, she collected herself and started to move towards the class of 11 years old. This class was facilitated by Andre. By the corridor only, the path seemed everlasting. All those memories she had been trying to suppress came to the surface, and Dhriti got lost in them - How much she loved her mother and how happy they were as a small family.

How she wanted to be a space scientist and explore the universe following her mother? How did she feel when her mother never returned from the space operation? How much did she suffer? How did her father step up and become her whole world? How her father was always there for her and never left her alone? His hugs, his smell, his touch... and she lost him forever! Tears started dropping from her eyes.

This trail of thoughts was immediately broken by Young Akshat asking, 'Dhriti Di, won't Andre bhaiya [2]come to the class today?' Suddenly, Dhriti realised she had already reached the class, sitting in her time capsule.

'Andre bhaiya is not well today. What if I take your class?' Dhriti quickly turned and wiped her eyes before Akshat could notice. She replied with made-up excitement.

Akshat ran into the class yelling, 'Dhriti Di will teach us today!'

The class started with excitement, yet it was about to be strenuous. It could be the first time Dhriti was simultaneously torn apart into two words. At the face, she was teaching the concept of a boiling point, but in her head, she was reliving the memories with her father and mother. The more Dhriti taught, the more she felt like disintegrating, but she couldn't help but continue. It was exhausting, but somehow, she was managing.

---

1 Respectful word for the elder brother in many Indian languages

To maintain the class environment, Dhriti added excitement by asking, 'So students, have you ever wondered if you could ever boil the water to a higher temperature than 100?'

'No, didi. It is not possible as water becomes gas at 100 degrees Celsius.' Said David and sat with the pride of knowing the answer.

'Wow! Somebody revise the chapters! But what if I say this "impossible" task is possible?' Dhriti asked with suspicion.

Hearing this, the students' jaws dropped in amazement. They started scratching their heads as this simple knowledge trembled the pillars of the facts they had gathered. They have always perceived that water would only boil at 100 degrees Celsius. It didn't feel less than magic to listen to this new information. Sensing the risen dilemma, Dhriti continued with a smile, 'Yes! It is possible.'

'But ma'am, how?' Asked the curly boy Huifen confusedly while rolling the virtual AI pencil in his hair.

'That is something you need to ask Andre bhaiya only.' Dhriti felt like teasing the curious souls.

'No, didi, Please tell us!' A unanimous voice came from the class.

While adjusting her hologram tools, Dhriti started an experiment in class: 'Don't believe my words; science is never about that. Let us see if the experiment supports what I said. So, here the temperature of the water is...'

'100 degrees Celsius,' David replied quickly.

'Exactly! We can see the water boiling, too. But when we increase the pressure in the apparatus, then... ' Students could see that the water stopped boiling. Still, the temperature remained at 100 degrees Celsius only.

'So, do you want to know how this magic happened?' Dhriti asked with a smile. The answer was obviously a unanimous, thunderous "YES!"

'Listen carefully! Every liquid has a boiling point, which is the point when it is converted to the gaseous state. However, it is dependent not only on temperature but also on pressure. Temperature and pressure are directly proportional to each other. This means that if we increase the pressure, the liquid's boiling point will also increase. Hence, any liquid, including water, could be boiled longer without being converted into a gas at a higher pressure. Which means...' Dhriti took a dramatic pause.

Young Zavi raised her hand and said, 'If we decrease the pressure, the water will boil at a lower temperature!'

'Exactly!' Replied Dhriti with newly gained enthusiasm. 'Water will boil at a lower temperature at lower...' Suddenly, Dhriti froze while teaching, but her lips still mumbled something. It felt like she had travelled to a different dimension, leaving her body, but suddenly she cried excitedly, 'Yes! Water will boil at a lower temperature at lower pressure. Water will boil at a lower temperature at lower pressure.' Instantly, unknowingly repeating the same line like a mantra, Dhriti left the class and started running towards the corridor. Her eyes were trying to find somebody as she checked other classes while running. The corridor headed towards the window from where she often experiences the sunset. Sensing the excitement of Dhriti, students felt as if it was an activity that was part of the class, and they started following her while speaking the same line – 'Water will boil at a lower temperature at lower pressure'.

As Dhriti reached the window, she found Sago alone, experiencing the sunset. Sago was about to ask why she was late for the sunset but was surprised to see the whole class running to him, following Dhriti. Seeing the students and Dhriti filled with energy and joy, Sago also started laughing. He could visualise the classical Pied-Piper story coming alive. Dhriti stopped near him, and while holding her breath and with the glitter of a thousand stars in her eyes, she said, 'I have found the solution.'

'What solution?' confused Sago asked Dhriti.

Elated, Dhriti replied, 'THE SOLUTION! I have found THE SOLUTION!'

The glitter in Dhriti's eyes was reflected in Sago's smile!

ooo

27

MISSION DESTROY ROBOTS

An idea can motivate you to an epitome, and motivation is a feeling that is inversely proportional to age. This means the lower the age, the higher one's motivation and excitement. As we get older, our "rational" thinking makes us cautious and ultimately makes us compromise on motivation. Henceforth, Yua and her gang's excitement was a natural thing. They were surprised that intelligent Yetis did not get this simple solution! But they remembered the golden words of Yeti Dada, "at times, common sense is not that common".

To further develop the plan, everyone decided to meet after story-time but secretly, under Yua's leadership. They agreed to meet physically and not virtually because the consequences would be unimaginable if the plan was leaked through any technology. The gang was very excited at the time of the storytelling session. A little happier than the regular days. They frequently made eye contact with each other and smiled or giggled. Yua tried to signal them not to do that, but they were young children only; how could they control one thing that they had an abundance of, happiness? Even Sago was surprised by this unusual behaviour but let them have fun without "adult intervention".

Ultimately, everyone met at their "secret place" as everyone dispersed from the story-time. Oscar started coordinating the meeting, 'Everyone, sit down quietly! Yua, what's the plan?'

Excited, Yua was just waiting to share the plan. It was a little unusual to see Yua in this excited state; to some, it was a little creepy seeing her this way. Yua started, 'So, first of all, tomorrow, right at this time, we will gather outside Guru Gyatso's room, from where we can keep an eye being invisible to Guru Gyatso. Dhriti di told me that we have almost every possible weapon there. Guru Gyatso would also be in his room at that time. So, we can just sneak in...'

Oliver intervened in Yua's excitement, 'But we will need the key to the room, which is Guru Gyatso's iris only.'

Electrified, Milani replied, 'I have the solution for this. In the morning, Gaurav and I will take a hologram picture with Guru Gyatso, and we can use the same picture as the key by zooming in on it.' Every eye in the room was raised towards Milani with respect and appreciation.

'Great, Milani, problem solved! So, in the evening, Milani, Gaurav, and Cloe will steal the disintegrating ray from the Guru Gyatso's hall. The weapon is big, so we need three children to handle it. At the same time, Oscar and I will go to the science lab to steal the teleportation ray…' Again, Yua's flow was disturbed, this time by concerned Cloe, 'But the science lab has a lot of people even at this time…'

'My acting skills can come to the rescue this time. I will act as if I am having nerve pain, like Andre bhaiya. That seems a serious problem, as even Yetis were very concerned about it. I will attract instant attention.' Oscar replied with pride with his first meaningful addition.

'Awesome Oscar, again, the problem is solved. So meanwhile, Oscar will diverge everyone's attention, I will steal the teleportation gun. We will all meet at this point at 10 at night, and without wasting any further time, we will attack the robot castle. No one will expect an attack in the night!' Completed Yua.

'But how will we reach there? We don't have their coordinates?' Asked sceptical Oscar. His question was critical and a reflection of his intelligence, especially as it was put by a ten-year-old.

'Don't worry, I only asked Abebe bhaiya this question a month back. I was keenly interested in knowing the functioning of the teleportation ray. The ray itself has major coordinates of the planet, and what could be more important than the Robo Castle!' Gaurav replied with excitement.

'Great! So, tomorrow night, we will meet here again at 10. Come with some tools for self-defence for yourself. Good night!' Said Yua, and the meeting was dispersed. Everyone was asked to leave the group in pairs or one by one. No one should get to know that a meeting was going on here.

The night was difficult for the gang. Some could not sleep due to excitement, and some due to anxiety. They had taken a task beyond their potential, but the upcoming reward was way too lucrative not to attempt the plan.

They could have misevaluated the intelligence and potential of both... Robots and Yetis.

ooo

28

THE PLAN

'Hail great mona… mona… monarch GR8001. Please permit me to enter your hall.' INOV8538 asked the monarch cordially.

'You are always welcome in my hall, my Scientist General. But what was the matter that made you come here physically? We could have connected telepathically.' Asked the monarch in his typical mechanical voice.

'The topic was like that, my master!' explained INOV8538 in an excited voice.

The enormous black door of the hall of GR8001 opened as the answer to the message of INOV8538. Before the main purple door of the hall, there was an endless corridor filled with sensors and lethal weaponry. With great power comes the great insecurity of losing it! A lot of changes have come to the monarch after having the LOE. Other than his raised ambition and inflated ego, his affinity for colours had increased. His insecurity soared even higher than his ambitions. Hence, he installed a plethora of advanced lethal technology for his rescue. This combination of ego, insecurity and unfathomable power turned him into a spitfire. Now, no other robot dared to see him, especially when he was angry. Even INOV8538 had a close shave with death in such times. Hence, if there ever was any bad news, he never risked sharing it by being physically present in front of him.

Soon, the green corridor ended, and he knocked on the main door, 'Sir, may I come in?'

'Yes, my General, welcome! Why are you here? How is the preparation of invading the planets of other solar systems going on?' Asked GR8001 inquisitively.

'Sir, the preparations are going fine. The range of the teleportation gun has also increased. By next month, we should be able to in… in… invade the only planet with a living population of the other solar system, and soon you will become the master of our gal…gal… galaxy. But there is something even more important than that…' Said INOV8538 with a thrilled voice.

'Are your circuits working fine, my science spearhead, or should I get them checked with a short circuit?

How can any news be more important than the reign of the Milky Way?' said the monarch in an annoyed, satirical tone.

'No, no master. Please pardon my idiocy. I was too excited about the news about human children…' said INOV8538 in a trembling, scared tone.

'What about it, my General? Two weeks back only, you informed me that the last lot of human children was over, and you were not able to manufacture the LOE on your own. The marks of that mistake are still fresh on your face… What other reward do you want for your achievement?' Said GR8001 in a sarcastic tone. This made INOV8538 touch the scars on his face once again. If SUGES8628 had not calmed down the monarch by reminding him of the relevance of the Scientist General, he would have gone dysfunctional then and there only. He was lucky that GR8001 hadn't reached the laser sword hanging from his waist this time just after listening to the news.

'The news deserves a definite reward, sir... I mean... you might feel like rewarding me... after all, you can only decide what to reward and punish with your impeccable judgment. Who are we to suggest...' The flattery calmed down the GR8001 a bit, and INOV8538 continued. 'Robo supreme, we have captured 5 human children outside your castle who were trying to snea… snea… sneak into the castle. The fools thought that they could do it with a teleportation gun. They didn't know how sup... sub... superior we... I mean, you are to them. Thanks to your visionary mind, we had teleportation jammers inside the castle. No one but the master can use teleportation in the castle.' Replied INOV8538 while fawning over the robo supreme. The last 2 weeks have been hell for him. Regular warnings have been coming from the monarch to complete the preparations to attack other planets. He had to put some water on this recently kindled fire against him; if not, he could burn alive with a single mistake. So, as the main guard of the castle told him about this news of capturing human children, he made sure to deliver the news to the monarch in person.

'Only five children? And you say this is great news! 538, your circuits seem to lose their place!' With this, GR8001 reached for his laser sword and put it on the mother-box of INOV8538.

'They have also shared the location of other abducted children after my intense interrogation, my lord!' INOV8538 said it in one go with lightning speed without any stutter or electric shock. Even a delay of a second would have made him dysfunctional.

The news was good enough to bring a smirk on the face of the monarch, with which he dragged the laser sword back and asked with a smile, 'Oh my scientist general, you must learn prioritization of sharing information. You saved your life with hardly a second.' The monarch sat on his throne and continued, 'Indeed, it is great news INOV8538. So, please tell me, my hyper-intelligent robot! Where are the rest of the mice hiding?'

'Where will a mouse hide sir? In her rat-hole in the mountains!' The news was enough to bring evil laughter to the lips of the monarch. Soon, the whole palace echoed with the horselaughs of the monarch and his General.

OOO

29

THE WAR

The weather is often calm before the most destructive storms. It was a sunny afternoon on the peaks of the Himalayas when, one after another, different teleportation portals started to open in the air. From these big portals began to emerge an unending line of hovering robots. Yua must have gone through a lot, from physical torture to psychic telepathy-based interrogation. God knows how they saved the critical information about the advancements of Yetis but couldn't save their location. GR8001 didn't want to take any risk. Hence, a plan was instantly made in the leadership of GR8001 & INOV8538. Within another 24 hours, a humungous army of robots equipped with deadly weapons was teleported to the snowy abode.

They expected as they will land on the Himalayas, they will find colonies of humans and Yetis. As the robots will see them, they will ambush, surround them, and make them surrender. Adding to human children, they will get Yetis as a bonus. Why did they think so? Because Yua and her gang fed them so. They didn't want to endanger others because of them. Hence, they shared that humans and Yetis have their primitive colonies, where they live in igloo-like buildings made of snow. They have put on an invisible protective shield that helps them from being discovered by anyone else. This seemed like a plot stolen from Marvel or DC comics of early-age humans, but what else did you expect from children? Anyway, what business did robots have with comics?

So, as the robots arrived on the snow peaks and started to hover over them, they got the shock of their life as they found nothing but snow. This made the GR8001 smile, as he had already planned for the solution to such surprise or shock. Today, the robo supreme was dressed differently, as if he had chosen this attire to annihilate humans from the Earth. A body fit suit of black colour laced with different kinds of most modern weapons along with a purple coloured cape. Right from his toe to his head were jewelled by lethal weapons of mass destruction. He was enough to finish the whole planet with this suit.

He gazed towards the pack of the five children. While scaring them of the glare of the laser sword, he asked, 'So, human children, where are others? Point at your colonies so that we can destroy the invisible protective shields.' As Yua heard this, her eyes started going red, and so did the others. Within seconds, there was a blast, and every human child blasted along with the robots holding them. None of the robots were prepared for this. They were trying to ambush, but suddenly, they realised they were stuck in a trap.

'Sir, they were not children but robots. This is a trap. Please abo… abo… abort the mission.' INOV8538 pleaded to the monarch. In the excitement of finding the human children, the Scientist General forgot to scan them to see if they were real children. Excitement can do this to you, overpowering logic and making you commit mistakes.

But with this sudden incidence, GR8001 has already gone into alert mode. He suddenly scanned the area around quickly, and with all the vision and weapon upgrades, GR8001 could observe the movement of a micrometre and destroy thousands of kilometres alone. He replied to INOV8538, 'Hush, my General! Traps are made for clown fishes, not for sharks. If they were really that brilliant, they could have attached stronger bombs to the same robots and could have blasted our palace while making them suicidal. But they didn't. They are low intelligence, naïve children, my General. Are you scared of small children?' General said while scanning and without making eye contact.

'Now, quickly scan this area through the microsatellites I asked you to prepare. Even an in should not be ignored.' GR8001's sarcastic tone transformed into an angry tone.

INOV8538 immediately surveyed the area with the machines but could not find anything other than the ocean of snow around them. He scanned multiple times, but the result didn't change. He also commanded other robots to recce the area, which also turned out futile. Finally, anxiously, he shared with the monarch, 'Sir, the machines are showing some life signs. But we are unable to find anything.'

This response made GR8001 angry, and he attacked a mount in his frustration with his sword, which immediately disintegrated into multiple pieces. 'What happened to your idiot machines? Have they started to perceive snow as humans, or have humans learned the technique to become invisible?'

At the same time, Dhriti, Sago, and others sitting at the science and weaponry centre of the Yeti world were observing everything happening outside. Due to the technology developed by Yetis, one could see outside of the mountains, but no one could see inside. Further, thanks to the technology mis-guiders, every signal of the robots' technology was reflected or started working erratically. Guided by their culture, Yetis have worked on one thing for a possible war, the defence. That was the reason that they never built big armies. But whatever was there was on the highest alert in the leadership of Gyatso with their disintegration rays ready. They were the only plan B they had. Yetis had taken a massive risk for humans, which was the least they could do within their limits.

Miss Dechen was taking care of the control panel today, and Andre was assisting her. Sago was standing with Dhriti in case he was needed, but Dhriti had been leading the project ideally until then. It was a beautiful scene of two species cooperating like cousins.

Observing the rising frustration of GR8001 and other robots, Dhriti signalled Miss Dechen to start phase 2 of the project.

Suddenly, a chuckle filled the valleys and peaks of the Himalayas, 'Ha Ha Ha, What happened, tin box uncle? Searching for something?' Robots were flabbergasted after hearing the voice but couldn't find its source. They started to look here and there to find the source but couldn't find it. It felt like the snow was speaking or the mountains had come to life. The confused robots looked like perplexed birds of old times, pigeons, searching for the voice source by looking everywhere in confusion. The voice came in again, 'Tin head uncle, you rightly said that machines are idiots. See! They can't even find a juvenile girl. Ha Ha Ha.' The chuckle continued with the voice of a 5-year-old girl.

GR8001, who was proud of the species of robots, felt deeply insulted by this remark. He yelled in his fuming voice, 'How dare you say this, you puny human! We are the epitome of evolution and intelligence.'

The innocent giggling voice replied, 'That is so visible right now, metal-head uncle!'

GR8001 hit one of the mountains with his laser sword in anger again. Seeing the situation getting out of hand, INOV8538 asked for permission to communicate further, which was immediately granted. 'If you have such confidence in your intelligence, then why are you hiding in these mountains?' asked INOV8538, trying to provoke the child to reveal herself.

The child's voice returned while echoing in the Himalayas, 'Because we wanted to stay away from the company of idiots! They say idiocy is contagious. Are you acting idiotic because of your idiot chief tin box uncle 2?'

Meanwhile, inside those gigantic mountains, everyone was focused on their task with full alertness, but they could not stop laughing. Yetis's belly pots were going up and down with heavy giggles. One young girl of 5 years was handling the mic and was given the immediate scripts by Sensei, who was himself in full action to write the provoking add-ons. Salma was working with both of them as an empathetic coordinator. Even a single mistake with the child could have been fatal to them.

The taunting and insulting conversation continued, and with every taunting remark marked by the girl, robots, along with GR8001, also started getting mad. Random attacks in the snow also became more evident by every robot. They commenced attacks on every possible place they thought the voice was coming from. The childish snowball attacks on robots started from nowhere in the mountains and enraged the robots.

It is not only a smile that is contagious; anger can also follow this flow. Seeing each other angry made the robots fume more and more. Eventually, the conversation reached a point when GR8001 yelled, 'You silly human puny child, get in my hand once. I will make sure you regret these giggles every day of your slavery. I will make you my personal slave, and once I flush out emotions from you, I will torture you every day! You will cry for death, but you will never get it!'

The giggling filled the mountains again, of not one but many children, 'Metal-head uncle, you are hilarious. But if you really feel so, then here I am. Come and catch me.' Suddenly, a girl appeared on the mountaintop. In his anger, the GR8001 fired a laser at her, but the girl got teleported to some other mountain before the laser could touch her. Again, the GR8001 targeted the girl and missed her. The monarch kept missing, and the girl kept being teleported. Other robots joined the supreme leader on his command but with the same result. Some of them even got injured by misfiring each other in an attempt to discover the logic of girl's appearances. The girl's appearance was planned to not have any pattern for this purpose only.

The robots started fuming with anger in the literal sense. Anyone could see them getting red and fumes coming out of them, anyone but them, as they were lost in rage.

Observing everything keenly, Dhriti suddenly spoke with excitement, 'Phase 3! Phase 3!' With that, Miss Dechen gently pushed a button, and a sudden snowfall started in the area. The temperature of the environment around them began to fall. Still, the temperature of the robots kept rising because of the anger. The vacuum pumps also started acting at the start of phase three. 'What the hell is this now? Is this your another trickery?' Yelled GR8001 with fumes coming out of his head.

The chuckle came again: 'Ohho! Robots, you are way more stupid than our expectations. This is Mother Nature, the supreme power, trying to cool you down.'

'No one can cool us down. We are the supreme.' Roared the robot supreme.

'If you are so supreme, then why don't you come and catch us? Seems you have become old and lethargic. Ok, I promise you we won't even move.' The innocent voice rechallenged the ego of the monarch. With these words, Dhriti yelled again inside the mountain, 'Open the gates!' This time, Gyatso pushed a lever, and the upper layer of the mountains started getting transparent. With this, the Yetis and children were visible, laughing and mocking the robots from inside the mountains. GR8001 has been waiting for this moment for more than one year now, but his anger has made him lose his mind. Rather than asking the humans to surrender, his ego, boiling with rage, yelled at its peak, 'FIRE!'

...and Bam! There was a blast, not inside the mountain but outside. One robot exploded! Within a microsecond, a series of explosions started, with every robot getting exploded by unbearable heat.

This sudden event made them angrier, and the explosion rate increased like anything. It was an unimaginable scene when every robot was blasting in the air automatically, as if someone had hidden a bomb in every robot that was timed to explode at this point.

Dhriti quickly signalled Miss Dechen to control the snow and Himalayas, given the rising temperature of these blasts. If not, a catastrophe would have hit the upper layer of the Himalayas and impacted the inside environment as well.

But how was that possible? How were Yetis & Humans doing it? What was the exact plan? There were many questions, but the answers were nowhere except with Sago & Dhriti. There was a smile on the faces of Dhriti, Sago, Miss Dechen, Guru Gyatso, Andre, and Salma, but others were shocked like anything. They felt as if a magician had played the best trick ever before them, and they were startled by that!

Suddenly came the most enormous explosion, almost equal to a devastating bomb getting fired with the body of GR8001 blasting and becoming ashes.

A colossal cheer started from inside the mountains, with random hugs and eyes filled with tears of triumph. The war was over—or at least it seemed to be over..

30

REVELATION

'"How?" This is the question in the mind of every Yeti and human child today. We know that the robot reign has been defied due to recent events. Still, it was a mystical strategy under which instantly the robots started blasting. We must have seen those 4D videos a zillion times on our holographic devices, with everyone either getting dumbstruck or trying to figure out the "how", but still, nobody knows how that happened? So, today we are here to discover this "how", and I request you, Sago Dada, to please answer this puzzle and satisfy our curiosity!' Asked the anchor Tashi to Sago.

This unforeseeable victory and viral holographic video of blasting robots have made Dhriti and the gang famous. Everyone was elated yet perplexed about the "how" part of it. Hence, Dhriti and the gang were invited to the central news channel of the Yeti world. Everyone over the globe was waiting to see the revelation part of the trick. Listening to the anchor's question, Sago replied, 'Tashi, if you want to know the "how" of any trick, then to whom should you ask, the magician or the assistant?'

Tashi laughed and said, 'Ha ha ha, obviously, the magician!'

Sago reciprocated the smile and replied, 'Exactly! And I am not the magician of this trick. It is our beloved Dhriti. So, I would request her to raise the curtain!'

Now, every eye was on Dhriti, who was sitting with the gang and other human students in a semicircle, with Sago Dada occupying the central seat. She had never been comfortable with so much attention, but the second name of assurance, Sago, was sitting along with her. So, she cleared her throat and started to speak, 'Before telling you the trick, I would like to ask you a question.'

The anchor was startled seeing the confidence of a young human girl but replied, 'Please go ahead, Dhriti.'

'What kind of grades did you get in physics in school?' Dhriti asked with a chuckle.

'Ha ha ha. I would say average. I mean, at least I never ran away from physics!' Tashi replied with a chuckle only.

'Great! So, you must be knowing the relationship between the boiling point, temperature, and pressure?' Asked Dhriti in a curious tone.

'I thought I was the one who was interviewing!' Tashi gave a witty remark and continued, 'OK. Let me try to remember. Temperature and pressure are directly related to each other...'

'Exactly! You are promoted Tashi!' Dhriti was giving competition to the anchor in wittiness. 'As you said, temperature and pressure are directly related. This further means that if we increase the temperature, pressure will increase, and the reverse will also be true. This is a simple and classical rule of physics and chemistry. Going by the same principle, the Himalayas are already a low-pressure zone. In a low-pressure zone, the boiling point of any liquid also decreases. For example, you can boil the water at low pressure to under 100 degrees Celsius.'

'Correct!' Anticipated Tashi. In a moment only, the whole world became the student of Dhriti, who continued further, 'Robots also had a liquid in them, the LOE, Liquid of emotions that they had extracted from humans. Robots understood only one part of emotions, so that they can increase perception and make one creative. But nothing in this world is entirely positive or negative; it is how you take it. Emotions are not an exception; if left uncontrolled, especially anger, frustration, and even despair can destroy you. We made the robots angry to the point that the liquid inside them started boiling with heat, but this didn't happen at a regular temperature. So, we lowered the pressure outside further with the snowfall and vacuum technology. Eventually, they started fuming and became nothing but a big pressure cooker of classic times that too without a whistle. More like a pressure bomb and blasted!' Said Dhriti and giggled like a child.

'Wow! So can we say that robots created the "Frankenstein Monster" out of the liquid they stole from humans?' Tashi asked while building on what Dhriti had said.

'Exactly! The last model of the robots was made after hundreds of years of improvement and had a perfect coolant for overheating. But as the robots stole the liquid from us recently, their body didn't adapt to this change. As Sago Dada says, "Any change takes time."' Said Dhriti, and everyone smiled with her.

'But what about those child robots that you used as bait? How did that idea come from?' Asked Tashi again.

This time, the answer came from even younger Yua, 'Actually, we eleven-year-olds also made a plan to defy robots…'

'Wow! You young children are so talented!' said Tashi, surprised.

'Ha ha, yes we are!' said Yua in her innocent voice, which made everyone laugh. 'But the plan was not that intelligent. We planned to steal the teleportation and disintegration rays and attack the castle with them. We even succeeded in stealing the guns…'

'Someone needs to improve the security.' Said Tashi and gave a look to Guru Gyatso. Everyone laughed again. 'Oh! Pardon me, Yua. What happened next?' Asked Tashi.

Yua started from where she left, 'The plan turned out to be too much for us, and we all got nervous. Oliver started crying only!' Other students started to point fingers at Oliver and started laughing. Oliver was trying to hide his face somewhere. With some chuckles from everyone, Yua continued, 'So, we decided to postpone the plan to the next day. Our plan was really demanding. What neither humans nor Yetis could do, we 10-years took into our own hands. Due to that, I could not sleep, and neither could Dhriti di. Eventually, I slept, but whenever I am stressed, I speak in my sleep and…'

'And you poured out the plan to Dhriti in sleep only? Oops! Thank god that you speak in sleep!' Saif Tashi and everyone laughed again.

'But a good oops. After that, Dhriti di got to know the whole plan, so she implemented the same with robots... with a little improvement. So, we couldn't implement what we eleven-years-old planned.' Yua ended with a sad tone, but it made everyone laugh, which brought a smile back to Yua's face, too.

'Wow! I know that I am saying "wow" too many times, but I am flabbergasted with this endeavour which has ended a universal threat for once and all. So, one thing that I am starting from today is managing my anger. Anger is really "danger"!' Everyone laughed again with Tashi's wittiness. 'So, Dhriti, What's next?' Tashi asked.

Dhriti paused and took a deep breath. 'Home!' Dhriti made eye contact with Yua and continued with wet eyes, 'Sweet Home!'

OOO

About the Author

ASHTAM NEELKANTH

In the late 20th and early 21st centuries, Ashtam Neelkanth emerged as a pivotal figure whose contributions would have lasting impacts on the realms of education and personal development. Known for his profound dedication to nurturing the potential of children, young adults, and emerging writers, Ashtam was much more than an educationist; he was a catalyst for change who transformed the lives of over 80,000 students.

During his time, Ashtam's work in cognitive and behavioural development transformed the lives of many. He guided students to become remarkable authors and thinkers, inspiring a generation to reach beyond the ordinary. His influence extended to various organisations, helping them grow and adapt in an ever-changing world.

But perhaps the most significant moment in Ashtam's life came when he experienced a powerful vision—a glimpse into a terrible future. Moved by this revelation, he felt an urgent responsibility to share his foresight with humanity. He transformed those visions into Beyond the Pinnacle, a work intended as a warning to guide future generations away from the mistakes he foresaw.

The warning went unheeded, and the consequences were profound. Ashtam Neelkanth's words now stand as a testament to the importance of his message, urging readers to reflect on the choices that shape our world and to learn from the vision he so urgently shared.